HOW IT WAS

HOW IT WAS
A Memoir of Samuel Beckett

ANNE ATIK

With Nine Portraits of Samuel Beckett
by AVIGDOR ARIKHA

Shoemaker S&H Hoard

First Shoemaker & Hoard edition 2005

First published in 2001 by Faber and Faber Limited
3 Queen Square, London, wc1n 3au

Grateful acknowledgement is made to the Estate of Samuel Beckett for
permission to reproduce copyright material on the following pages: pp. 5, 8, 9,
10, 23, 26, 27, 28, 30, 31, 32, 38, 39, 43, 46, 47, 50, 51, 56, 63, 64, 65, 69, 74, 75, 81, 84,
87, 90, 98, 99, 103, 107, 109

Library of Congress Cataloging-in-Publication Data
Atik, Anne.
How it was : a memoir of Samuel Beckett / Anne Atik ; with nine portraits of
Samuel Beckett by Avigdor Arikha.—1st Shoemaker & Hoard ed.
    p. cm.
Originally published: London : Faber and Faber, 2001.
ISBN 10: 1-59376-087-6
ISBN 13: 978-1-59376-087-8
1. Beckett, Samuel, 1906- 2. Authors, Irish—20th century—Biography.
3. Irish—France—History—20th century. 4. Atik, Anne—Friends and associates.
5. Paris (France)—Biography. I. Title.
PR6003.E282Z5638 2005
848′.91409—dc22   2005028810

Shoemaker [S&H] Hoard
An Imprint of Avalon Publishing Group, Inc.
Distributed by Publishers Group West

Printed in the United States by Malloy

10 9 8 7 6 5 4 3 2 1

HOW IT WAS

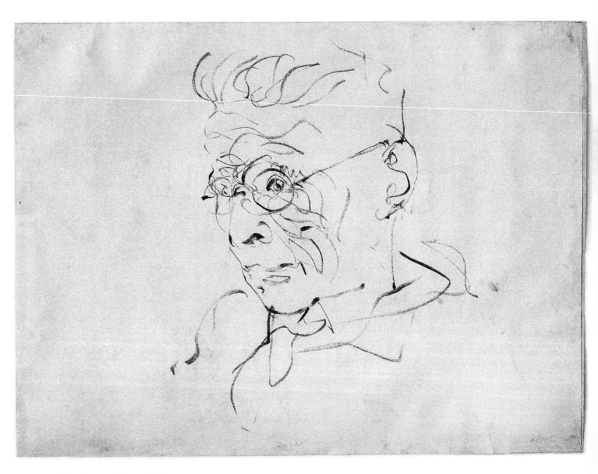

1 *Samuel Beckett, 20 May 1965.*
Crayon on paper, 29.5 x 40 cm.

AFTER fifteen years of memorable conversations with Beckett, I realized that I could not depend on my memory. The unforgettable was becoming the irretrievable. It would have broken our friendship had I taken notes in his presence. I wanted to, of course, and, of course, I didn't dare. It was clear from the very first time I met him in 1959, as it was immediately clear to anyone who met him, that this single-minded, intense, erudite, passionate and above all truthful man, beautiful to look at, was inhabited by what used to be called the 'divine afflatus'. I finally started taking notes – and even then not regularly – in 1970, stopped, then started again, from 1974 on, usually just after he'd left our house, or on returning from a restaurant.

Which leaves out all the years and mostly nights spent at the Falstaff, a bar-restaurant on rue du Montparnasse, or at Chez Françoise in the Invalides, La Closerie des Lilas or the Iles Marquises, or at La Coupole, where, before I met Sam, he and Avigdor, not yet my husband, used sometimes to meet for lunch as well as drinks. Nights when we'd drunk too much for me to write anything at all (as an American just out of milkshakes and the regulation Chianti); evenings which sometimes lasted till four in the morning, whiskey alternating with wine, capped with a few beers, crowned by champagne.

They drank up and down the Boulevard Montparnasse, Avigdor and Sam – his companion, Suzanne, never joined us – chummily bobbing along in full fettle, Sam assuring Avigdor too solemnly, and too late, as they lurched onwards: '*Wein nach Bier das rat ich dir; Bier nach Wein das rat ich kein*' – 'wine after beer I can advise, beer after wine would not be wise' – towards the Dôme, where they often ran into or avoided Giacometti (because of his harking back to the same, albeit remarkable, story each time

3

they met, about the revelation he experienced while sitting in the cinema le Cinéac, as to the difficulty of perceiving and drawing) – myself in a state of near collapse.

No quantity of alcohol, however extravagant, seemed to affect their memory, either for historic dates or for poetry, and the two had gone on in this way since their first conversation in 1956, when Avigdor was twenty-seven years old and Sam fifty – even if the long drinking sessions became shorter and more manageable over the years, and getting up in the morning less of a struggle.

And though their memory was phenomenal, each relied on the other to supplant what had been left out. Often Sam would ask A. what year it was when such and such a play or prose piece or poem of his was first published or produced, or even written, since A. knew so much of his work by heart. He in turn remembered A.'s every exhibition, every painting. His visual memory was striking; he remembered paintings of Old Masters which he'd seen in his travels through museums in Germany, France and Italy, those in Ireland and England, their composition and colour, the impact each one had had.

This made him that rare phenomenon among writers in that he had a visual culture, and spoke of painting past or present in terms used by the pictorially articulate, shortening the distance between *pictura* and *poesis*: terms like 'space', 'form', 'light', 'surface tension', etc., lifting or lowering his hands to show which part of the canvas he was referring to, much as he did when describing music. In the catalogues from museums in Dublin, London, Dijon, Kassel, Munich, Dresden, Berlin, Vienna, Milan, and so on, all of which he gave A., there are scattered annotations which bear witness to an attentive, passionate viewer, and in his work he referred, sometimes indirectly, sometimes directly, to these paintings, positioning his actors and actresses accordingly: the staging of *Not I* was inspired by the composition of Caravaggio's *The Beheading of St John the Baptist* which A. had urged him to see when in Malta, at the cathedral of La Valletta. The idea of having only a mouth on stage preceded his trip to Malta; but once there, Sam was

2

4

2

Selmun, 25.10.71

Chers amis – Merci de votre lettre du 22. Le courrier de Paris ne met pas trop longtemps. Mais d'ici l'acheminement doit se faire par canot à rames. Vu cette formidable peinture à Valetta (co. Cathédrale de St. Jean). Très difficile de trouver une reproduction même aussi moche que celle-ci dénichée à Mosta. Il y a aussi un St. Jérôme avec Crâne. Tout continue à bien se passer. Temps très beau. Nagé trois fois aujourd'hui. Personne à l'hôtel. Conduite (automobile) sans histoire. Visité Gozo. Vu la grotte de Calypso! Attribution soutenue par certains spécialistes. Sinistre antre. Sacrée nymphe. Bravo pour Los Angeles. Réforme vite les Beaux Arts et sus à la peinture, resus. Continue mollement la traduction du Dépeupleur. Beaucoup de mal. Peri-arthrite [?] toujours pareille mais plus supportable. Comprendre qui pourra. Vin local buvable. Celui de Gozo excellent. Trouvé du Tullamore Dew à Mellicha.

Affectueusement à vous, Sam

Selmun, 25.10.71

Dear friends – Thank you for your letter of the 22. The mail from Paris doesn't take too long. But from here it has to be transported by rowboat. Saw this marvellous painting* at Valletta (co. St John's Cathedral). Very hard to find a reproduction even as awful as this one dug up at Mosta. There's also a *St Jerome with Skull*. All continues to go well. Beautiful weather. Swam three times today. Nobody at the hotel. Driving (automobile) without problems. Visited Gozo. Saw Calypso's grotto! Attribution upheld by certain specialists. Sinister den. Hell of a nymph. Bravo for Los Angeles.[†] Reform the Beaux-Arts quickly and go at painting, *resus* [resurrected]. Continuing without much enthusiasm translation of *Dépeupleur* ['The Lost Ones']. Hard going. Peri-arthritis still the same but more bearable. Make of that what you will. Local wine drinkable. The one from Gozo excellent. Found Tullamore Dew in Mellicha.

Love to you both, Sam

* Caravaggio, *The Beheading of St John the Baptist.*
† A.'s scheduled exhibition at the Los Angeles County Museum of Art held in 1972.

5

deeply impressed by the dichotomy in the composition of the Caravaggio: the kneeling figure on the left and the curious but indifferent onlookers on the right. After his return from Morocco, he told us about a figure sitting absolutely still while apparently listening to something or someone in El Jadida. He then chose to reverse the composition for the play: inspired by the immobile posture of the Arab woman, he placed the indifferent Onlooker on the left and the mouth on the right.

* Alte Pinakothek, Munich.

* National Gallery of Ireland, Dublin.

Another instance is the positioning of May's arms in *Footfalls*, modelled on Antonello da Messina's *Virgin of the Annunciation**; or Ter Borch's *Four Spanish Monks** with the hat on the table, where one seems to be intruding on a meeting in a Dutch painting, and which A. surmised to be the origin of the staging for *Ohio Impromptu*.

Sam also confided in A. about new work, and many *pneumatiques* sped back and forth with questions and reactions, in mutual exchanges. (Before the fax, the *pneumatique* was a system whereby letters were propelled by air pressure in suction tubes linked to post offices in each *arrondissement*. They took two hours from sender to receiver and were easier to conserve.) At some point during the 1950s Sam showed A. a text about a man and his pocket, which he referred to as *La poche*, then abandoned, but which later led to Winnie's bag in *Happy Days*. During that period he also showed A. a short piece provisionally titled *Balfe* (in his childhood there had been someone by that name), but then abandoned that, too. Many years later, in 1973, A., remembering *Balfe*, asked Sam if he could use that text for a book of his prints which a publisher had proposed doing, and Sam agreed. The volume, now out of print, became *Au loin un oiseau* (*Afar a Bird*).

In the summer of 1956 Sam invited A. to his country house in Ussy and let him read something he was in the midst of writing, which was to become *Endgame*. (At that time, the monologue was still not written.) Sam merely referred to it as *la petite pièce*. A few weeks later Sam wrote to him saying that he was '*très touché que la petite pièce vous accompagne ainsi. Le problème du titre me tracasse toujours. J'ai l'impression qu'il faut éviter le mot "Fin".'* ('[I'm] very touched that the short play stays with you so. The problem of the title still bothers me. I have the feeling I should avoid the word "End".')   3

That was also the year Sam brought A. the classical Cassirer edition of Kant, so heavy that Sam asked him to change the location of their rendez-vous from a café to A.'s flat, *'vu le poids… d'Emmanuel'* ('in view of the weight…of Emmanuel').   4

But it wasn't only Kant that he'd brought, though Sam wasn't aware of this. Four years later, in 1960, at one of the appointments made by *pneumatique* to meet for dinner at the Closerie des Lilas, A. brought along a manuscript which he'd found tucked into one of the eleven volumes of Kant. The manuscript was called *Petit sot* ('Little Fool').   5

Sam was not very interested just then in the text which A. had found – though Kant might have appreciated the irony of Pure Reason protecting a Little Fool. He dismissed it as not very good; it was his first poem in French. A. later typed it up in two copies, nonetheless, one for Sam and one for himself, which he kept with the original manuscript.* (Two lines – *vont lentement lui enlever/ lentement les blanches heures* – suggest a poem by Apollinaire, *'Comme lentement passent les heures'*, which he loved and recited often.)

Neither was Sam happy with *More Pricks than Kicks*, but gave the galleys to A. anyway. Sam hadn't wanted it to be republished (but was finally pressured into giving permission). When Richard Seaver of Grove Press later saw the galleys at our flat, he said he'd never got them back from Sam.

In spite of, or rather along with, those exchanges, quips, questions, there were also entire evenings when he didn't say a word. At such times it was not easy to break the silence; it would have been worse than interrupting an avowal. There'd be a murmur, a

* It had to do with Sam's earliest conscious feeling of guilt: an innocent act in his childhood, when about five or six, of putting a hedgehog into a shoe box to protect it from the cold, providing it with worms, and finding it dead one morning. He told us that story several times, it weighed on him throughout his life, and found expression in *Petit sot*, which was expanded later.

4.9.56   Ussy

Cher AA
    Merci de votre lettre. je suis très touché que la petite pièce
vous accompagne ainsi. Le problème du titre me tracasse toujours.
J'ai l'impression qu'il faut éviter le mot "Fin".

    Lindon a été absent de Paris tout le mois dernier et je n'ai
pas pu lui reparler de votre projet. Mais je lui en avais déjà
parlé. Il est maintenant rentré et vous pourriez aller le voir de
ma part. Téléphonez-lui aux Editions de Minuit, BAB 34.97.

    Je suis sérieusement fatigué et voudrais rester à la campagne.
Mais cela ne sera pas possible et je pense être à Paris vers la
fin de la semaine prochaine. je vous ferai signe. J'aimerais
beaucoup voir votre travail.

    Bien amicalement à vous.

Sam Beckett

je n'ai pas votre numéro de téléphone

merci de vos cartes du Nord.

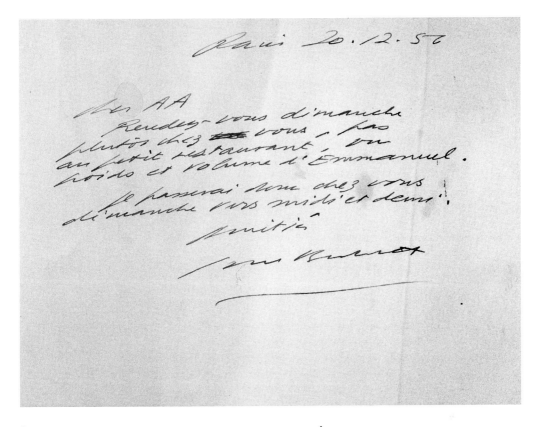

3
Ussy, 4.9.56
Dear AA

Thank you for your letter. I am very touched that the little play stays with you so. The problem of the title still bothers me. I have the feeling that the word 'End' must be avoided.

Lindon* was away from Paris all last month and I couldn't speak to him again about your project. But I have already told him about it. He's back now and you can go see him in my name. Call him at Editions de Minuit, BAB 34.97.

I am terribly tired and would like to stay in the country. But that won't be possible and I think I'll be in Paris by the end of next week. I'll let you know. I'd very much like to see your work.

Kindest regards
Sam Beckett

I don't have your telephone number. Thank you for your cards from the North!

* Beckett's publisher at Editions de Minuit.

4
Paris, 20.12.56
Cher AA

Rendez-vous dimanche plutôt chez vous; pas au petit restaurant, vu le poids et volume d'Emmanuel.

Je passerai donc chez vous dimanche vers midi et demi.

Amitiés,
Sam Beckett

Paris, 20.12.56
Dear AA

Rendez-vous Sunday rather at your place than at the small restaurant, in view of the weight and bulk of Emmanuel.

I'll pass by your house at about twelve-thirty.
As ever yours,
Sam Beckett

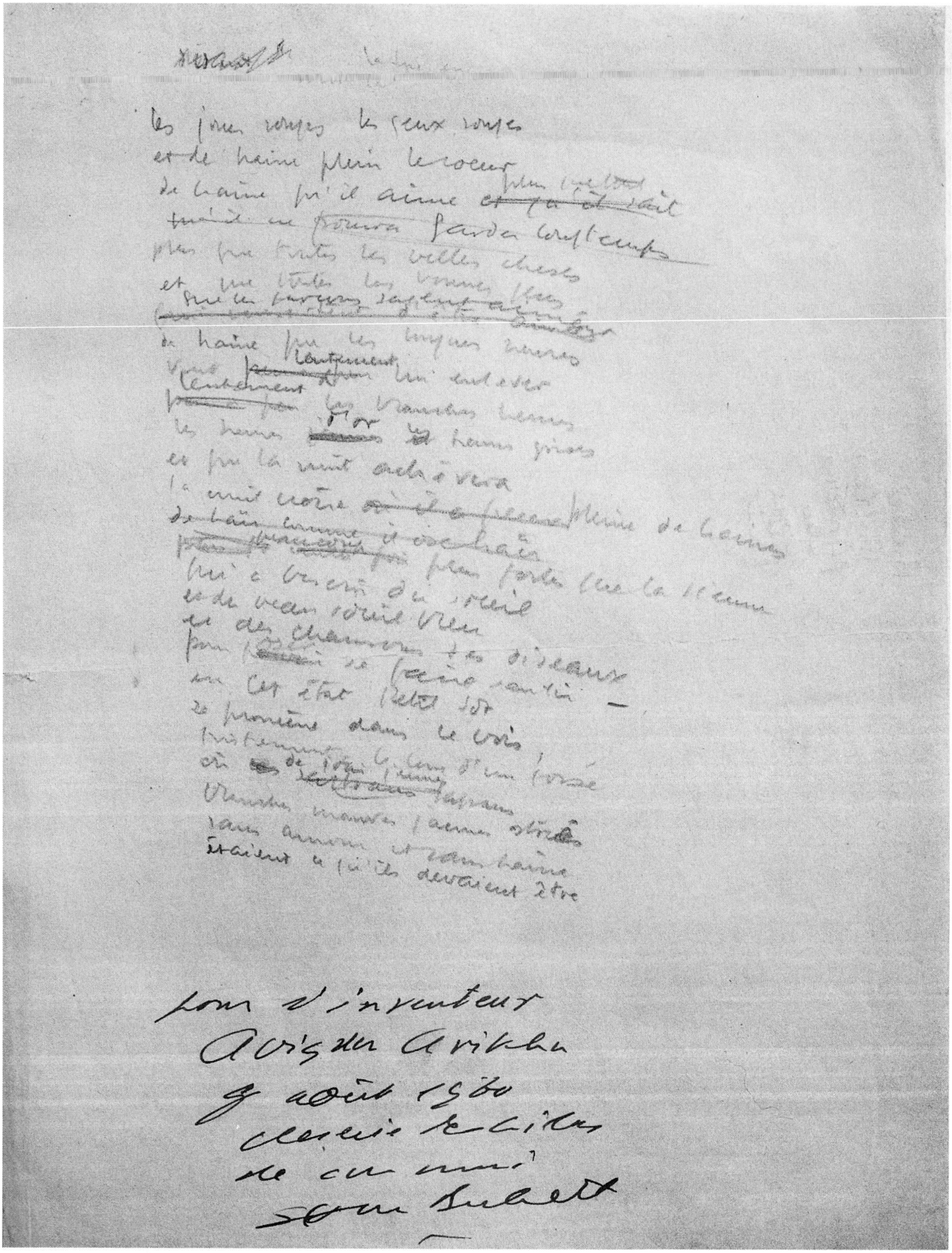

5 Manuscript of *Petit sot.*

shift in position, and someone's voice slowly breaking the artefact that silence had become. Even though Sam's was not an aggressive silence directed against anyone, but rather a sinking into his private world with its demons, or so we imagined, those present suppressed their acute discomfort and feelings of ineptitude when it happened. His intimate friends learned how to cope with his struggle – A. by talking about a wine he had tasted, the theatre designer Jocelyn Herbert by bringing in a chessboard.* I coped by bringing up Dr Johnson, and Con Leventhal, his old friend from Dublin, by retailing a bit of Trinity College gossip. They, or we, coped by doing any of the ordinary things friends do, the more ordinary the better, to bring to an end the fleeting and rather frightening chill.

Precisely because no one could so enhance one's sense of being listened to, and people aren't used to being wholly listened to, these moments of chill made one feel personally responsible, even guilty. Years later I came upon a text I had read and mentioned to Beckett, who then had only nodded his head, whether in agreement or discomfort I couldn't tell: 'R. Zeev of Strykov says: "He who is silent when he has nothing to say is not taciturn – the truly silent man is the one who remains quiet when he has something to say...I remain silent, and whenever I am tired of remaining silent, I have a quiet rest, and then go back to being silent."'

Eventually we learned not to take it personally. But each time it came over him it was like being in a tunnel with someone dear whose face you suddenly couldn't see. Or who couldn't see you.

There were always other people at the Falstaff, which became a sort of club: when Con Leventhal, Sam's oldest friend and another inveterate drinker, moved to Paris, he would often join us, together with his companion, Marion Leigh; so would Sam's nephew, the flautist Edward Beckett, who had come over to study in 1961, and who, young as he was, and being of good Irish stock, learned to hold his liquor. We saw Edward frequently from the time he began his studies at the Conservatoire, where he took first prize in 1965. We would sometimes meet at the Rosebud, further up, on the rue

* Sam, an avid chess-player, would sometimes play with Jocelyn's mother, Lady Herbert, herself no mean player. He played games by correspondence with several people, including the journalist Kobler in the sixties; he had also played with Marcel Duchamp in the thirties, among many others. He followed the chess championships passionately, replaying the moves at home.

6 *Samuel Beckett, with glasses on the forehead, 7 January 1967.*
Brush and ink on paper, 27.8 x 20.7 cm.

Delambre, where, in that inexplicable way in which one hang-out is preferred to another down the road, many writers living in Paris congregated. But the Falstaff remained one of Sam's favourite haunts and hence that of his friends and admirers. Some of these may have drunk as much as they did in order to mask their reverence, to make their meeting less of a *levée* and more of a convivial evening's get-together.

Among those in attendance from time to time was Patrick Bowles, a very open and kind man with literary ambitions of his own, but who did not say much in the presence of Sam. He had translated *Molloy* (though Sam later redid it) and was a more reasonable night-bird than the others at the Falstaff, or at least when we were present. There was Richard Seaver of Grove Press, who had translated *La fin*, and his wife, Jeanette, the musician, of whom Sam was equally fond.

One of the quirkiest of all these was Patrick Waldberg, much younger than Sam. They had met in the thirties through their mutual friend, Georges Duthuit.* Waldberg, a very cultivated man and, though American in origin, a true Parisian, was also a Surrealist (a group about which Sam had nothing good to say, except for some of the poets initially associated with it and whom he had translated, such as Paul Eluard, René Crevel and André Breton himself). Waldberg was a *bon vivant*, but irritable, very touchy indeed, often roaring drunk, and a great billiard player, as was Sam. A. and I once went along to watch them play at Les Mousquetaires on avenue du Maine, which still exists. Sam tried, at first eagerly but then only for form's sake, to get A. interested in billiards, but it was no go. A.'s focusing was such that he could barely play ping-pong. I could play ping-pong but could not control the billiard cue. Patrick could do both expertly but could not disguise his astonishment, let alone his disdain, at our clumsiness. It was his nephew, Edward, with whom Sam most frequently played billiards at Les Mousquetaires.

Yet communication between Sam and A. remained coherent; sometimes slurred in the early mornings, to be sure, but not week-in, week-out. What made them instant friends, I suspect, was

* Matisse's son-in-law, art historian and the editor of the revived review, *Transition* (the pre-war *transition*), and with whom Sam had collaborated on *Three Dialogues.*

7 *Samuel Beckett with a cigar, 1970.*
Etching and aquatint, 30 x 23.5 cm.
1st of 2 trial proofs of the 2nd state. No edition,
plate accidentally destroyed. (London, The British Museum)

not only their love for German literature, but their shared thirst for knowledge in general, their passion for and, at the same time, wariness of erudition; erudition was their temptation, what Cicero was for Petrarch, and both knew it sometimes was come by at the expense of innocence.

Both remembered what they talked about at their first meeting, in 1956 – examples of theatre which A. had seen in an Arab village. This was backstage after a performance of *Godot* directed by Roger Blin at the Théâtre Hébertot. (A. had met Blin in 1950. Blin invited him for a beer one day, the two sat down, Blin lifted his glass, and said nothing at all during the entire drink – perhaps because he stuttered – but A. followed suit, the prototype for many such silent evenings he was later to spend with Beckett.) The friend who had brought A. to meet Beckett that first evening kept kicking him in the shins, trying to signal something: A. did not know then to whom he was talking. It was only when Beckett had left that she told him. A. was invited to meet him three days later, on 2 July 1956, in any case, at the poet Alain Bosquet's house. But Bosquet also invited ten other people, mainly writers. Coming in the door, Sam saw the company, then noticed A.; he went over to sit by him and they drank nearly half a bottle of whiskey together. Sam enjoyed describing this scene to me. Bosquet had arranged – incredibly, knowing Sam – for the whole party to go on after dinner to the Crazy Horse Saloon, a high-class striptease nightclub, but the two of them, after walking with the others and popping in to the club for a minute, popped out again and walked and talked until eight in the morning. (Someone later sent A. a catalogue, anonymously, listing a letter from Sam which had been sold in 1977 to an autograph dealer, G. Morssen, in which Sam thanked Bosquet for that evening and for introducing him to 'Arikha', *'que j'ai trouvé fort sympathique'* ('whom I found very likeable'). It was sold by Bosquet himself, who needed the money to buy a letter by Arthur Rimbaud!)

It was during this early period (1956–7) that both the Berliner Ensemble and a production of Nō theatre came to Paris, and

A. urged Sam to go and see them. (Beckett's plays have been compared with some aspects of Japanese theatre.) Sam was recalcitrant about going to the Nō performance, so A. acted out some scenes for him; for instance, rowing across the living room as the actors had rowed on stage: without moving, by grasping and dipping imaginary oars, in accordance with their principle of economy; enacting their movements indicating the passage of time – seasons, battles – by a few gestures of the hands; he described the drama of the empty stage; the reduction of colours to black and white. But Sam didn't go. However, he did go with Suzanne to see *Galileo Galilei*. He was impressed by Brecht's staging, said he liked the scene with the mirror, but found it all *trop riche*.

Some years after I met Sam, A. decided to cut out all alcohol except for wine; he'd noticed a few brown spots on his hand and took these to be a warning, calculating that he had drunk about enough to fill a small pond, or was it a lake? But Sam was horrified. How would A. get through the evenings? (Once, at about 3 a.m., someone at the Falstaff gave Sam one glass of champagne too many which he at first tried to refuse, then good-naturedly poured over his head.)

Nothing in my background could have prepared me for the huge role alcohol played in these people's lives. I did not try to keep up with them; in fact I didn't like whiskey very much and learned to order the bitter Fernet-Branca instead, which rather amused Sam, who'd order it for me in an extremely serious voice before I even sat down, or ventured to order mineral water – but then everything I came across in Paris was so different from what I had known in New York that I simply took it to be part of the scene, a given, like the Seine. So Sam's drinking as much as he did at the time – lessening a bit later on, though not at the end – did not shock me; his purity and gentleness wove it all together. A great poet, of Irish stock, who liked his drink, and that was that. And though sometimes drink-happy, he never appeared drunk.

8 *Samuel Beckett with a glass of wine, 7 October 1969.*
Brush and sumi ink on Japanese paper, 26 x 33 cm. (London, The British Museum)

When A. stopped smoking in 1963, Sam's trepidation had been even more pronounced. 'But what will you do?' he asked in bewilderment. Nevertheless, A. managed to get him to change from cigarettes to small cigars, and since we still brought him whiskey or cigars, as did visitors, and as we enjoyed his enjoyment (and enjoy them he did, all the way to the end, at the age of eighty-three), he was reassured. The only question was would it be Scottish malt or Irish whiskey, Jameson's or Power's, or even Bushmill's, from the North.

The circle around Sam expanded over the years, with smaller tangential circles. These included Barbara Bray* (whom, after Sam's introduction, we used to see a lot of, who was always helpful, and

* A script editor and member of the drama team at the BBC involved in commissioning *All That Fall*, and important in Beckett's life. See Knowlson, *op.cit.*

whose English sentences were as neat and compact as her handwriting), and later Jocelyn Herbert, when she came to Paris or we went to London. Sam had a special regard for Jocelyn, professionally and personally: she was an anchor of integrity, common sense and tolerance, as those working with her still appreciate. He was always very relaxed around her. There was a small but wonderful party at Jocelyn's house in 1973 after a performance of a double-bill of *Krapp's Last Tape* and *Not I*, which Sam had directed himself, with Albert Finney as Krapp and Billie Whitelaw in *Not I*. There were many people from the Royal Court, friends and family as well as other writers and actors. Sam was in a bubbly, champagne mood, jovial in a way he could only be with English-speaking friends, and played the piano in Jocelyn's dining room. After he'd finished a piece, a popular one as I remember, Antonia Fraser, who was there with Harold Pinter and looking beautiful and bridal, said smilingly, 'I can't help myself, I've got to say it: "Play it again, Sam."'

But essentially, our greatest evenings were spent as a threesome.

It took six years after their first meeting for Sam and A. to address each other in the *tu* form, and they both remembered when 'it' happened. In spite of Sam's evident affection, A. would never have proposed it himself. It is a serious step, one that implies an intimacy and trust that has been tried and tested – but many Americans find all barriers to immediate intimacy bewildering, if not off-putting and undemocratic. By the time they took that step I was around, and it was easier for Sam to address me in the *tu* form when we broke into French.

When A., twenty-three years younger than Sam (and thirty years younger than Suzanne), had told him in November 1960 that we might get married, Sam said that when we did, he'd marry Suzanne. He had mischievously formulated it as though it were a dare; actually they married six weeks before we did. Once he had decided, he went about it carefully and discreetly. James Knowlson covers this event as fully as can be expected in his indispensable biography of Beckett, *Damned to Fame*.*

* James Knowlson's invaluable, nearly exhaustive – and the only authorized - biography, *Damned to Fame*, Bloomsbury, London, 1996, passim

Although she never accompanied us later on, Suzanne used to go out with Sam and A. until a month after I arrived. If the three of them did not go out, she would make dinner in their flat at 6, rue des Favorites. A. remembers her as being very health-conscious: the first meal he ate there was of sardines, rice and lettuce. (Later, when things were easier, smoked salmon alternated with sardines.) Sam and Suzanne bought their food at a health shop she'd discovered on the rue de l'Abbé Groult, not far from their flat, years before the popularity of organic food; I think they started to do this after the war. She was the first person I ever met who drank black-radish juice. (I have since learned it contains many minerals, especially sulphur, beneficial to digestion.) Sam once made lunch for us at his new flat in Boulevard Saint-Jacques – to which I arrived half an hour late because I couldn't find the way – also of delicious smoked salmon, a small salad, wine. On that occasion he talked about Fritz Mauthner, whose work on linguistics he was interested in. The friend who had introduced me to A., the philosopher Gershon Weiler, had written about Mauthner.*

Suzanne and A. sometimes went to the theatre when Sam didn't go, or to concerts. On one of these evenings, shortly after A. and I had begun to see each other and he'd arranged to meet me after the concert, he looked at his watch. Suzanne understood the gesture, and may have been slightly put off. It may have been one of the reasons she invited him less often after that. She was also quite upset when A., as a housewarming present for their move to Boulevard Saint-Jacques, brought them three whiskey glasses of thick crystal commissioned from a crystal-cutter. In Sam's background there had been such things to please the aesthetic sense, but not in hers, and though a generous person capable of great courage – as she proved during the war – she frowned on luxury. (She used to enjoy shopping at the flea-market – Sam was rather proud of her finds; in later years he often wore a brown beret she'd picked up there. He was a meticulous dresser, and this beret didn't fit him, making his ears stick out, yet Sam liked it very much, especially

* Thereafter, whenever Mauthner's name came up, Sam would ask casually, but with evident curiosity, how Weiler was and if I still heard from him – an instance of Sam's interest in people's relationships.

19

in cold weather – or she would sew things for herself and for others, which for a time had been their means of support.) She was a woman of austere habits. *'Je suis une abbesse'* ('I am an abbess'), she used to say.

As for those late nights, perhaps she was simply being cautious, especially of his English-speaking friends with whom he stayed out so late and from nearly all of whom she kept a cold and frankly hostile distance. We wondered if a more fluent English would have enabled her to limit the liquefaction, so to speak. The friends they saw together were mostly French-speaking. Sam's nephew Edward was a beloved exception to all these generalizations. He spoke French to one and English to the other. He had learned some French at school, but put this to practice only when he arrived in Paris at the end of August 1961. Sam was touchingly solicitous. He was deeply attached to his family and felt very responsible for his brother's son, talking often before his arrival of what had to be done to make him feel at home. For his first week Sam had arranged for Edward to meet with the actor Jean Martin and Martin's friend, a painter called Manolo Fandos, to help him brush up on his French. They looked after him and took him out in the evenings, but he also went out with Suzanne and the writer Robert Pinget, the composer Mihalovici and his wife the pianist Monique Haas, the designer Matias, among the friends Sam and Suzanne had in common. Suzanne adopted Edward warmly, and so did we, as did all who met him. Suzanne did not associate Edward with the English-speaking contingent, and was on cordial terms with other members of Sam's family.

At the time I met Beckett I had just started learning French, so the poets whom we recited then – he, mostly, by heart – were mainly English-language (although he and A. would break into French from habit), Yeats above all. As my French improved, they would both recite French poets (many of whom Beckett had translated) and then, feeling less restrained, German, Italian, Spanish and, once A. had told him about Pessoa, Portuguese, which Sam studied in order to read him in the original. But especially German. Since A. also remembered poems in Swedish (by Erik Lindegren) and Spanish (by Neruda, mostly) and both of them knew other Spanish poets, and Sam's Italian was excellent, the liquid and labial, guttural and glottal sounds issuing from the two of them in all these tongues were like the cymbals, horn and bass in an orchestra.

And music, precisely, was our greatest bond; poetry was part of that bond, the other half of the heart, as it were. Our evenings at home began with music, before dinner, and ended with music, with poetry in between. Sam would tell us what he wanted to listen to that evening, or we'd put on new recordings, sometimes piano music that he – or he and Suzanne – had worked on at home.

Early on in our acquaintance we listened to Mozart and Beethoven, especially the chamber music (Sam wrote a television play called *Ghost Trio*, where the Largo is as important as the two actors on stage); sometimes Chopin or Webern, but Bach rarely – 'I haven't reached it yet,' he offered in explanation. Mostly we listened to Haydn's late string quartets – and then, invariably, to Schubert. A. could not understand why he didn't take to Bach; nor, once I joined them, could I. Was it that his architecture and resolution emerged from a certainty about the world? About time? That there was Eternity? A certainty Sam could never agree to, but which was the firmament over Bach's century – and certainly his soul? This occurred to me later as a possible explanation of his attitude to Austen.

In about 1964, Sam came with his cousin, the conductor and composer John Beckett, and there ensued a fierce discussion about Mahler's symphonies; John, A. and I loved them, Sam didn't, said about them, 'There's too much in there'; this is what he'd said about Wagner's music, too. Such an outlook was totally consistent with his outlook in general on writing and painting: he preferred economy. Economy was grace (which may have been why he preferred Webern – whose music could hardly be described as exaggeratedly lengthy – to Berg). So,

9
Ussy, 14.5.66
Cher Avigdor,
    Je t'ai vu fauché en rêve:
    Ne m'enguirlande* pas.
    Embrasse bien Anne et Alba.
    Affectueusement,
    Sam

Ussy, 14.5.66
Dear Avigdor,
    I saw you broke in my dream:
    Don't bawl me out.
    Give my best love to Anne and
Alba.
    Love,
    Sam

* 'Enguirlander' is a euphemism for 'engueuler', to reproach, tell off.

* An argument for 'the proof of the truth of fiction': this goodness one finds in some of the archetypal figures Dickens's genius created – Samuel Pickwick, Joe Gargery – but that Beckett actualized in his person. Beckett's own genius created twentieth-century archetypal figures, such as Winnie – of stoicism etc.

trying to change his mind a few years later after listening to a short piece by another composer as a prelude – but I have forgotten who that was – we put on the record of Mahler's Fourth symphony in A.'s atelier, our daughter Alba, only a few months old, propped up on the table in a sit-up chair as we listened, she along with Sam, John Beckett and his first wife, Vera. We all listened for fifty-seven minutes. At the end, it was clear that no one had given an inch.

We listened to it, incidentally, on a new hi-fi which Sam had left outside our door, aware that the old set A. had had for years was whimpering and literally going to pieces. This was his fairy-god-father side, demonstrated again, for example, towards Tophoven ('Top'), his German translator, who, Sam learned, was having trouble breathing due to an old wound – this was in the seventies. Sam immediately sent Top a 'breathing machine' like the one he used for his respiratory problem.

No one mentioned in these pages, nor anyone who had anything to do with Sam, even for five minutes, could fail to be struck by his sheer goodness. It came to him as naturally and unself-consciously as blinking, as swallowing.* Which is what made his friends so very protective of him, with a protectiveness considered by onlookers as over-reverential. Anecdotes about his goodness border on hagiography. His being a Protestant saved him from being a saint, but he would definitely have been considered a *tsaddik*, a saintly man (whose few failings made him wonderfully human) revered by the Hebrew tradition, and no doubt other religious traditions as well. He manifested his uncanny sense of people's distress in unexpected ways, as when he sent A. a cheque one day in the mail, with a note saying he'd dreamed that we were broke. Just then, we were! (A. was able to repay it a few weeks later.)

Even at the very beginning of their friendship, in the fifties, A. remembers Sam turning to him (they were on the platform of the Number 62 bus) and saying, '*Si vous êtes fauché, dites-le moi, car j'en ai maintenant*' ('If you're broke, tell me, because I have some money now'). He actually didn't have

Aarg 14.5.66

Cher Vigdor
    Je vais en famille
et rêve.
    Ne m'engueulande pas.
    Embrasse bien Anne
et Alba.
        Affectueusement
            Sam
            —

very much then, but some of his books had been selling better than expected. There are innumerable instances of such gestures towards other people; he often caught them by surprise, and they, too, remember him asking, off-handedly, as though it was an afterthought, 'Are you all right for money?'* For himself he didn't much care and would dismiss our remarks about his tin *deux-chevaux* Citroën (which he had chosen with the help of the Canadian abstract painter Jean-Paul Riopelle) with a laugh.

* As does Christopher Logue in *Prince Charming*, Faber and Faber, London, 1999, p. 235.

Once he believed in someone's work, he was tireless in doing what he could to get it known. There were the writers Marguerite Duras and Robert Pinget, the painters Henri Hayden and the brothers Bram and Geer van Velde, not to speak of Jack Yeats, whose work he first saw, and loved, in Ireland. Sam's championship of A.'s work started early when it was still abstract – he hung a huge abstract painting he bought from A. opposite his bed. With Bram van Velde and Henri Hayden as intermediaries, Sam tried to interest their dealers in A.'s work – but the dealers were puzzled and impatient: the chemistry wasn't right. Luckily, soon after, other dealers became interested.

But then he gave up abstract painting, for which he'd become well known in France, in order to draw from life – a move regarded as revolutionary in 1965 (not surprisingly, in view of the modes prevalent then) – and the ensuing years proved difficult. Sam himself was at first taken aback by this new direction, but once convinced, enthusiastic. It was the painting of the shoes that settled it for him, he said. Again, Sam tried to help in finding a dealer who might be interested. He thought of one he'd known many years before, back in 1948, Aimé Maeght, for whom he'd written the introduction in the series *Derrière le miroir*, numbers 11 and 12, discussing the Geer and Bram van Velde exhibitions. (Sam was also a good friend to their sister, Jacoba, a writer, whose eyes were the same brilliant blue as her brothers'.) Sam contacted Maeght and brought along a big, heavy portfolio of drawings, having arranged with A. to meet at a café afterwards on the corner of Boulevard St-Germain and rue du Bac.

It suddenly started to rain heavily, and A., waiting on the corner, saw Sam running towards him with his jacket off; he had wrapped it around the drawings to protect them, and was himself drenched, with no hand free to wipe the rain from his face. '*Ça y est, je crois qu'il a été accroché*' ('That's it, I think he was hooked,' or, 'I think it'll click'). Not only had it not clicked, but Maeght, wanting to seize an opportunity, wrote to Sam asking him to supply a preface for Saul Steinberg instead, with no mention of A. Sam did not reply.

Exceptionally, he even endured a dinner given by the gallery owner Claude Bernard for A. after the opening night of his drawings show there, in January 1967, for which Sam had written the first small text '*Pour Avigdor Arikha*'. We could see it was difficult 10–15 for him, but he was as stalwart as a soldier.

By far the most telling moment, the most fraught with tension, was towards the end of 1965, when Sam tried to interest Pierre Cabanne, then the art critic for the newspaper *Combat*, in A.'s work. Sam organized a visit to the studio with Cabanne, Robert Pinget and his old friend from the Ecole Normale and Trinity College, Georges Belmont.

A bit of bustling about; canvases brushed against each other and, falling, picked up; conversation forced; Sam's face taut but his manner studiously nonchalant. A., defensive, taken aback by what he assumed was a lack of interest, but controlling himself, showed a few abstract paintings so quickly that not more than a glance could be had. He then mumbled that he only drew from life now and showed a few drawings. Nothing more said, polite noises made, Sam grimly and unsuccessfully still trying to be casual, Cabanne looking lost. He left after a while.

Five years later, in 1970, Cabanne recalled this scene in a review of A.'s drawings show at the Centre National d'Art Contemporain which had just opened. In the first paragraph he began by saying how the drawings had left him with a feeling of uncertainty, how the meeting had ended in confusion; then, to Cabanne's everlasting credit, and to Sam's

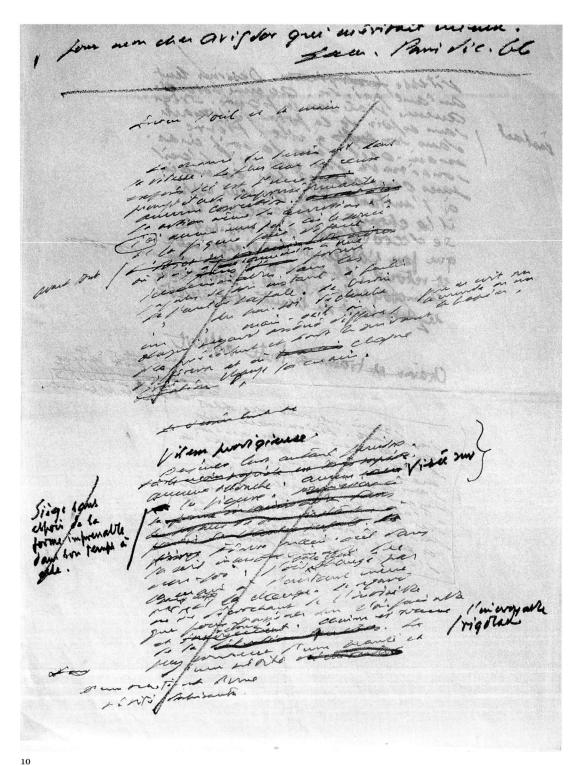

10

Pour mon cher Avigdor qui méritait mieux. Sam, Paris déc. 66

For my dear Avigdor who deserved better. Sam, Paris Dec. 66

First and second versions (French) of text for A. A.

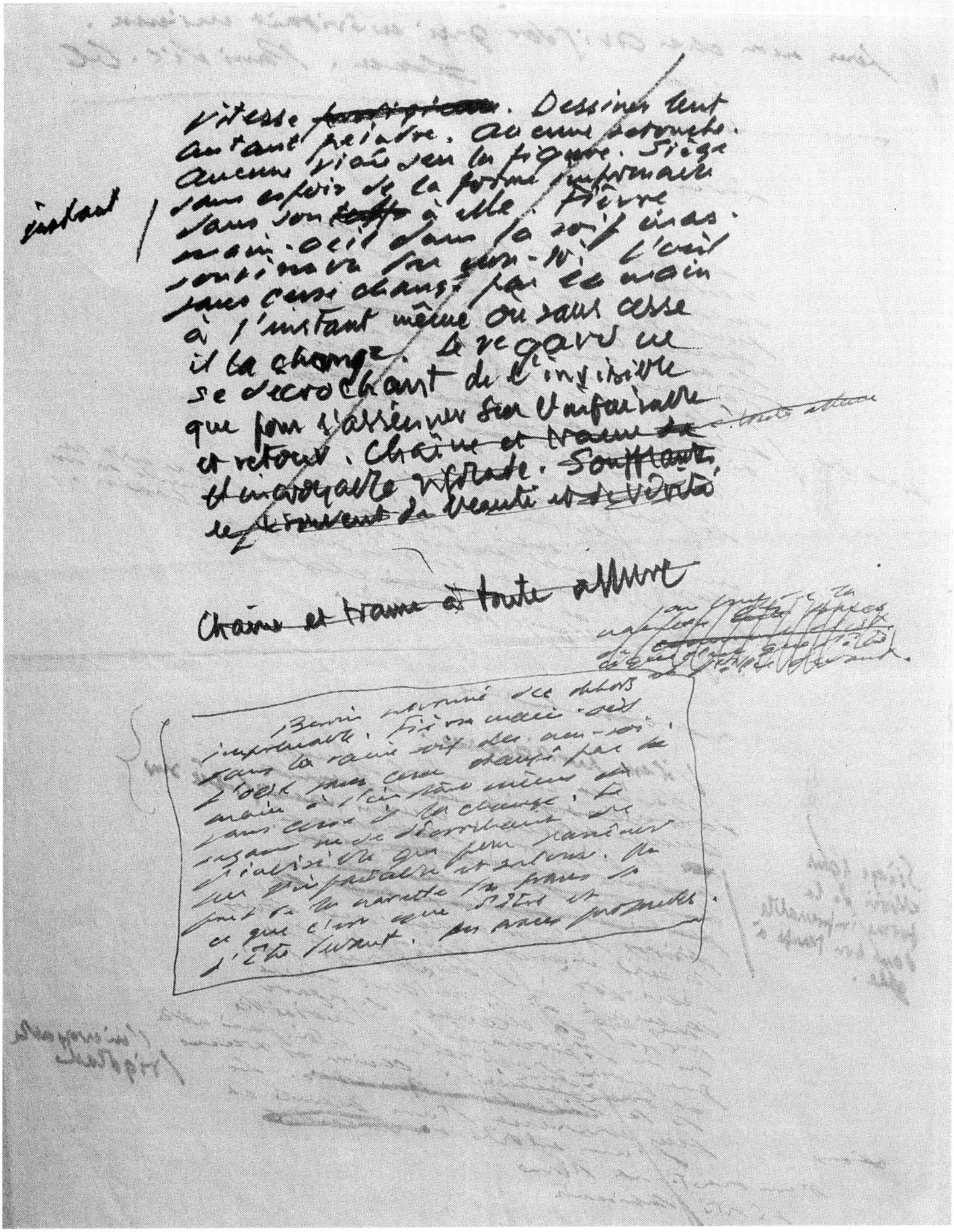

11 Third and fourth versions (French) of text for A. A.

Besoin retrouvé du dehors imprenable.
Fièvre main-oeil dans la vaine soif du non-soi.
L'Oeil sans cesse changé par la main à l'instant
même où sans cesse il la change. Le regard ne se
déprenant de l'invisible que pour s'asséner sur
l'infaisable et retour. Au bout de la navette
des traces de ce que c'est que d'être et d'être
devant. Des traces profondes.

Besoin retrouvé du dehors imprenable.
Fièvre oeil-main dans la soif du non-soi.
Oeil par la main sans cesse changé à l'instant même où sans cesse il la change. Regard ne s'arrachant à l'invisible que pour
s'asséner sur l'infaisable et retour éclair.
Trêve à la navette et traces de ce que c'est
que d'être et d'être devant. Traces profondes.

12 Fifth version (French) of text for A. A.

For Avigdor Arikha

    Recovered need of the impregnable
without. Fever of hand and eye in a
thirsting after the not-self. The eye
without ceasing changed by the hand
at the same instant as without ceasing
the hand by the eye. The look releasing
the invisible only to pounce on the unmakable and back without pause. Sus-
pension of the shuttle and traces of
what it is to be and to be in face of.
Profound traces.

                Samuel Beckett

13 Last version of text for A. A. before
the correction sent from Lisbon.
(Letter on page 30.)

HOTEL AVENIDA PALACE
TELEG. PALACE · TELEF. 30154 · LISBOA PORTUGAL

25 - 12. 66

Cher Avigdor

J'aimerais changer
la première phrase du
texte en :
"Siège remis devant
le dehors imprenable"
Si tu es d'accord
et s'il est pas trop
tard.
Nous avons fait un
bon voyage. Il fait
du soleil. Nous partons
maintenant à
Cascais près d'Estoril

Affectueusement
à vous deux

Sam

14

Lisbon, 25.12.66

Cher Avigdor

J'aimerais changer la première phrase du texte en:
'Siège remis devant le dehors imprenable.'
Si tu es d'accord et s'il n'est pas trop tard.
Nous avons fait un bon voyage. Il fait du soleil. Nous partons maintenant à Cascais près d'Estoril.

Affectueusement à vous deux
Sam

Lisbon, 25.12.66

Dear Avigdor

I'd like to change the first sentence in the text to:
'Siège remis devant le dehors imprenable.'
If you agree and it is not too late.
We had a good trip. It's sunny. We're leaving now for Cascais near Estoril.

Love to you both
Sam

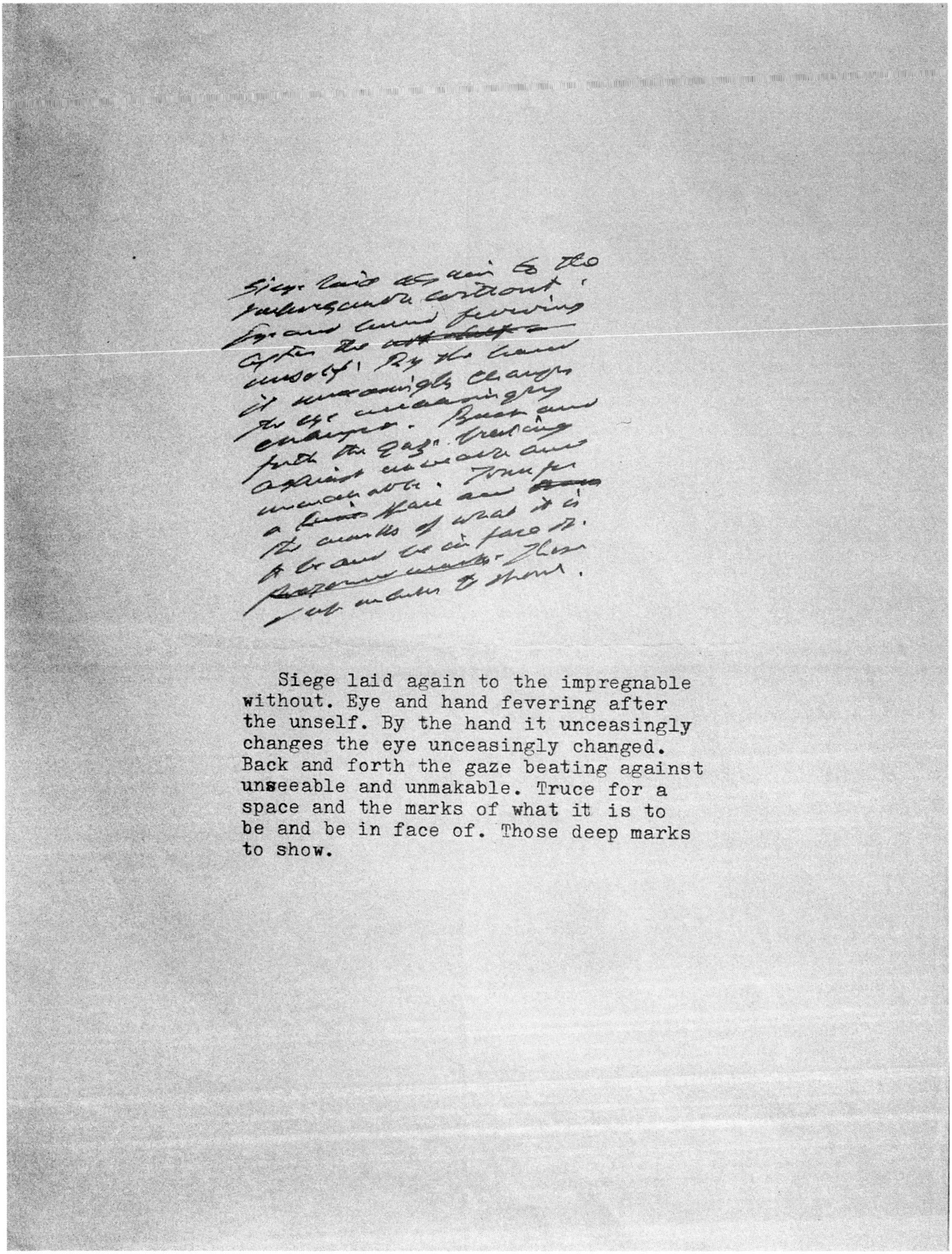

[handwritten manuscript text, partially legible:]

Siege laid again to the
impregnable without.
Eye and hand fevering
after the unself. By the hand
it unceasingly changes
the eye unceasingly
changed. Back and
forth the gaze beating
against unseeable and
unmakable. Truce for
a space of what it is
to be and be in face of.
[illegible] Those
[illegible] deep marks to show.

    Siege laid again to the impregnable
without. Eye and hand fevering after
the unself. By the hand it unceasingly
changes the eye unceasingly changed.
Back and forth the gaze beating against
unseeable and unmakable. Truce for a
space and the marks of what it is to
be and be in face of. Those deep marks
to show.

15 First English (final) version of text for A. A.

mollification, after writing: 'First impression: disappoint-ment...Five years ago I saw these drawings, couldn't make them out,' etc., he went on to say, 'But I was wrong'; how Arikha drew like nobody else, etc. A nice day for journalism, a nice vindication for Sam – who'd been appalled at the way things turned out at that meeting.*

Anyone who knew Sam well knew that his generosity did not stem from a deprived childhood for which he was trying to compen-sate; on the contrary, his early years had been happy, fortunate. He would even ask, uncomprehendingly, why people thought his writings must mean he had a miserable childhood. All they have to do, he added, is go to the window, read the papers, it is all there. A. remembers being with him in a taxi, stopped at a traf-fic light, and Sam, looking out the window, suddenly throwing up his hands and murmuring, almost to himself, *'La détresse, la détresse'* ('Distress, distress').

He loved his father, and told us several times, lingeringly, about the long walks they took together; furze and gorse were often in his vocabulary, indelibly part of his landscape in childhood and in the work. But he also told us about the time when, a young boy, he was taught to swim by his father. In order to learn, Sam had to dive into the cold sea from the rocks at Sandycove. His father had said, from below, holding out his hands, 'Jump. Trust me.' And frightened as he was, he did jump, but he still remem-bered the height and the fear, and repeated how his father had said, 'Jump. Trust me.' That initiation and those words remained with him, and the tone of voice in which he told us showed how deeply it had struck. (And he became a very good swimmer!) The bond between him and his father, and with his family in general, was very deep.

One cannot explain away his generosity as a compensatory act. Simply, it stemmed from a visceral compassion that started in his ears, listening to the hints people inadvertently dropped about their condition, which led straight to his pocket. As men-tioned before, Sam listened intensely to everything that was

* But there was a curious reaction from A.: as I read this review and other very posi-tive and even glowing ones aloud, he sat gloomily curling his hair, his face getting paler and paler, turning almost green the more enthusiastic the reviews; when I asked him why, was he ill, it can't be because of the critics, he replied, 'Maybe my work is shit.' That sounded like Sam.

said to him, no matter how trite, to the point of throwing his interlocutors off-balance when they realized what they were saying. We read in a newspaper, probably after Sam's death, how one day in the 1970s he was recognized by a student on the Boulevard St-Michel who engaged him in conversation; Sam, surmising that the student could not pay his hotel bill, went there in his absence and paid it anonymously. No one else could have known about his financial difficulty. This article was probably written by the student himself.

Not all hints were inadvertent, however; magnanimity naturally reached sharper ears, and these also led to Sam's pocket. There were some sorry instances of spuriousness, which Sam didn't care a damn about. Knowlson quotes Sam telling him that although he knew some individuals were not really hard-up, 'I can't take the risk.' One would-be writer, who in turn became a would-be draughtsman, rented a flat near to Sam's apartment building so as to waylay him in the street, which he did, looking adroitly sorrowful, showing him some drawings, and ending up with some of Sam's clothes and some money, as Sam himself told us, matter-of-factly. Sam brought him to the flat to show A. his work, about which A. preferred to say nothing. There were many others, and many methods were used to play on his guilelessness. But Sam would very much have minded the churlishness of these last few lines. He himself didn't care, and in fact looked for ways of getting rid of his money, especially after the Nobel Prize, telling his friends he had lots now, that he could help them out, as he had even before the Nobel whenever a book sold well. They in turn would have to convince him that they were solvent and really didn't need anything.

In this he resembled a very dear friend and patron of A.'s, Alix de Rothschild. She also knew when people were putting on the poor mouth in her presence, but didn't care. She preferred to lose rather than make a fuss. It got so bad that both Alix's and Sam's friends began to refrain from even mentioning money. So alike were they in their *noblesse de coeur* that in the evening of the opening of A.'s drawings exhibition, prefaced by Sam, at the

16

34

CNAC, A. asked the two of them to come to a buffet in our house along with a few other friends. Sam never accepted social invitations unless with intimate or at least familiar friends, but for A.'s sake, he did. Alix was tall and thin and beautiful; Sam was tall and thin and beautiful. As though they were alone, they formed a sort of twosome. Sam stood, she sat, and they talked with that ease we ascribe to aristocrats, completely comfortable with each other, like people who had known each other for years. In a sense, they had: we had been telling each about the other for twenty years. They never met again, but always asked after each other.

Sam's happy childhood no doubt accounted for the unforced tenderness which he demonstrated towards children in general, not least towards our daughters. Alba was his god-daughter (though, being Jewish, we had nothing to do with the Church, which no doubt suited Sam just as well); at her birth he'd given her his baptismal spoon, and a few months later a coral teething necklace. (I seem to remember him referring to this custom in connection with Dr Johnson or Johnson's time, but can't trace it.) We called her Alba after his poem of the same name. He bought her the most elegant pram in the shops (I don't know who went with him, or bought it on his behalf, or if he went by himself), and the biggest teddy bear in Paris, or so we thought as we tried to get it into her room (he remembered loving his teddy bear, Baby Jack, as a child); also tiny doll-sized boots from Corsica, and, for her first birthday, the original edition of *How It Is*. He watched her grow with great attention. For her second birthday he gave her the manuscript of *Le dépeupleur* (*The Lost Ones*),* and when she was thirteen, the manuscript '*il fut trouvé par terre*'. (That same year he gave our younger daughter, Noga, the manuscript of *Un endroit l'attire*.)

When she had trouble falling asleep, as many three-month-old infants do, we used to put Alba's cradle near the drawing board posed on a trestle on which we ate. On one such occasion, impatiently wanting to take part in the two men's conversation, I

* At some point neither Sam nor his publisher, Lindon, could find the manuscript of *Le dépeupleur*, but fortunately A. had photocopied it, and so could send it to Sam from Israel.

16 Sam, Anne and Alba at A.'s opening, Centre National d'Art Contemporain, Paris, 8 December 1970.
Photo © André Morain.

17 Sam, Alba and Anne,
Ussy-sur-Marne, August 1966.

chanted, 'Oh, please go to sleep, please go to sleep, for the honour of France' – and Sam sang out, 'and Navarre!'

Sam had a magical touch with children. He never patronized or talked down to them, never criticized or baby-talked, but was always completely natural, talking about cricket matches, swimming, homework, teachers, with the same complicity and empathy he evinced towards old friends. If, later on, they remembered their encounters with him as slightly awesome or uncomfortable, this was because the parents were fluttering apprehensively around the room – parents like us, for example – afraid of wasting Sam's time, of trying his patience, afraid of the children saying anything banal.* There were times, though, when he did feel tired, depressed, or anxious about his work. He often apologized for his mood, even though no one referred to it.

* Our children felt that tension when we listened to music together; especially Alba who, as a teenager, was keen on pop and rock as well as 'classical' music. They were both too young to know Sam as other than our close friend. But he inspired a certain awe in them all the same, as Noga remembers.

18

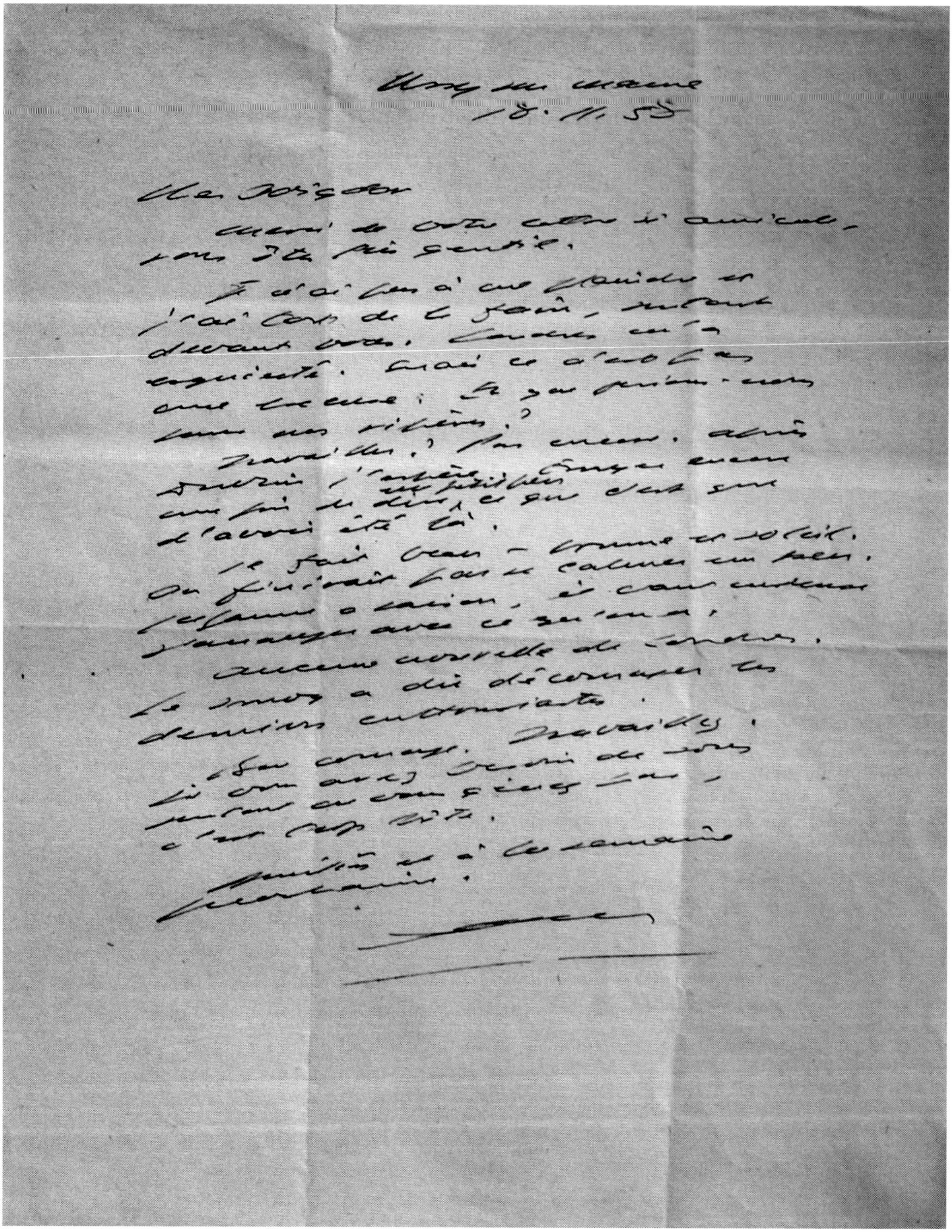

Bourg en Bresse
18.11.53

Mon Directeur

Merci de votre lettre si amicale,
vous êtes très gentil.

18

Ussy sur Marne, 18.11.58
Cher Avigdor,

Merci de votre lettre si amicale. Vous êtes très gentil.

Je n'ai pas à me plaindre et j'ai tort de le faire, surtout devant vous. Londres m'a esquinté. Ce n'est pas une excuse. Et que pourrions nous sans nos misères?

Travailler? Pas encore, après Dublin j'espère. Essayer encore une fois de dire ce que c'est que d'avoir été là.

Il fait beau – brume et soleil. On finirait par se calmer un peu. Suzanne a raison, il vaut mieux s'arranger avec ce qu'on a.

Aucune nouvelle de Londres. Le smog a dû décourager les derniers enthousiastes.

Bon courage. Travaillez. Si vous avez besoin de sous surtout ne vous gênez pas, c'est trop bête.

Amitiés et à la semaine prochaine.

Sam

Ussy sur Marne, 18.11.58
Dear Avigdor,

Thank you for such a warm letter. You are very kind.

I have nothing to complain about and I shouldn't complain, especially to you. London has worn me out. That's not an excuse, and what would we do without our problems?

Working? Not yet, after Dublin I hope. To try to tell one more time what it is to have been.

Weather fine – mist and sun. I will calm down by and by. Suzanne is right, it's better to make do with what we have.

No news from London. The smog must have discouraged the last enthusiasts left.

Bon courage. Work. If you're broke don't hesitate to ask, that would be too silly.

As ever yours and see you next week.

Sam

Beckett held the idea of the 'professional' poet in abhorrence. To him it was virtually a contradiction in terms. Craft, structure, rhythm, linguistic energy were assumed prerequisites, but poetry was a calling, not a profession, not something you could *decide* to do at a certain moment. He meant what Keats meant, whose work he knew so well, when he wrote that 'if poetry comes not as naturally as the leaves to a tree, it had better not come at all'. He certainly did not mean that poets should not earn money – he himself had taught for a while (was miserable during that time), had translated prolifically, written essays and reviews – but that the *poem itself* should not be academic or intentional, that the library shelves must not crush the furze. Beckett was a poet down to his teguments, ligaments, cells; standing or sitting, poetry's presence in his presence was as pervasive as oxygen.

His way of reciting poetry was at the polar opposite of the French school of declamation. In reciting, Sam would sing, or croon, reading Apollinaire's refrain *'voie lactée'*, from *La chanson du mal aimé*, in the same line intervals as a blackbird's song. When I continued to read aloud other lines from the same poem, he corrected the way I read by singing-crooning them.* This goes against his very own insistence on keeping colour out of his actors' voices, asking them to keep it flat – 'too much colour, Billie [to the actress Billie Whitelaw], too much colour,' meaning to leave off acting, and instead to transmit the structure of the sentence, the pace and musicality of the words themselves, the power of what was being said or left unsaid, made to function like pauses in music. Even the syllables of the names of the characters were counted: in *Godot* the ratio is 3:2 – Estragon, Pozzo, Vladimir, Lucky – and in *Endgame* all four characters have names of one syllable adding up to 'Hammer' and 'Nail': Hamm (hammer) and Clov (*clou*, the French for nail); Nagg and Nell, *Nagel* (nail in German). In that play, too, the monologue appears between two other movements, like an adagio in music.

* *Mon beau navire, ô ma mémoire*
Avons-nous assez navigué
Dans une onde mauvaise à boire
Avons-nous assez divagué
De la belle aube au triste soir

(Loosely and inadequately translated: 'My lovely ship, oh memory/ Have we sailed enough/ In an unsavoury wave/ Have we raved enough/ From dawn till dreary eve')

By far the most memorable instance, in A.'s memory, of hearing Sam's work 'straight from the oven', occurred on 20 December 1956. This was one of the greatest spiritual, aesthetic discoveries in A.'s life, which he never tired of describing, and which can never tire because the words always have the same effect that art has on the body, the sudden chill and increased pulse that Keats and Housman and Nabokov tried to describe. In August of that year, while A. was visiting Sam in Ussy, Sam had first shown him an as-yet-untitled version of what was to become *Fin de partie*. Then, in December, when Sam brought a suitcase full of books to A.'s studio in Villa d'Alésia – the Cassirer edition of Kant's works in eleven volumes, as mentioned earlier – he sat down on the huge grey couch and said, 'I've added a monologue,' without specifying '*la petite pièce*', but meaning that part of the almost-finished *Fin de partie*.

A. asked, 'If you know it by heart, can I hear it?' And Sam began to recite what is surely one of the great monologues in twentieth-century drama: '*On m'a dit l'amitié, mait c'est ça, l'amitié...*' When he continued, '*Je me dis...*', going from major to minor, A. burst into tears; in Beckett's English translation it is just as wrenching, just as musical: 'They said to me, That's friendship, yes, yes, no question, you've found it. They said to me, Here's the place, stop, raise your head and look at all that beauty. That order! They said to me, Come now, you're not a brute beast, think upon these things and you'll see how all becomes clear. And simple! They said to me, What skilled attention they get, all these dying of their wounds.' And then, the sudden, stunning inversion in counterpoint: 'I say to myself – sometimes, Clov, you must learn to suffer better than that if you want them to weary of punishing you – one day. I say to myself – sometimes, Clov, you must be there better than that if you want them to let you go – one day...'[*] He referred again to the play later, one evening, saying he'd call the play *Fin de partie – Endgame –* which prompted A. to ask if it was a continuation of Mr Endon's unfinished chess game in *Murphy,* and Sam said he hadn't thought of that but yes, it was. In 1984, A. designed the setting and costumes for the New York

* From the Faber and Faber edition, 1958.

41

* Film and theatre director and founder of the Samuel Beckett Theater in New York.

19

20–21

* Sam's approval, therefore, especially after he'd seen the mock-up back in Paris, came as a confirmation.

* The publisher of Grove Press.

* Knowlson, *op.cit.*, p .525.

* Mary Bryden's *Samuel Beckett and Music*, Clarendon Press, Oxford, 1998, goes into greater detail.

production directed by Alvin Epstein, who also played Hamm, with Peter Evans as Clov, James Greene as Nagg, Alice Drummond as Nell, and produced by Jack Garfein* for the new Samuel Beckett Theater, before going on to the Cherry Lane Theatre. Over the phone A. described the scenery to Sam in Paris; adding that it was based on the golden mean, which excited Sam. (Sam was very good in maths, and used it often to work out the staging of his plays, the relationships between steps; indeed, to work out the probabilities of people's encounters and failed encounters.) He said it sounded fine. Which was a relief, because A. had designed a set that rejected *misérabilisme*, and conceived it in greys, not in black, to indicate a trace of the life that had been lived there, the faces of Nagg and Nell parchment colour, Hamm and Clov powdered white.*

There was a grand party in New York after the inauguration of the Samuel Beckett Theater, and favourite 'Sam' stories were told, including the one Barney Rossett* told about Sam waiting for the Rossetts to wake up (which Knowlson also describes) which took place in 1964 when Sam was shooting *Film* with Buster Keaton (and for which A. had suggested using the Sumerian god Abu as one of the pair of eyes following the protagonist around).*

Sam's way of reading aloud, reciting, set the bar very high for his actors. They all ended up imbued with the music of his texts. Nor is it any wonder that so many composers were attracted to his work: Mihalovici, Dutilleux, Berio, Heinz Holliger, Philip Glass, Morton Feldman, John Beckett...*

Alberto Giacometti came ringing the bell at 10 Villa d'Alésia one day in 1957 (A. had no phone), to tell him that Stravinsky, whom Alberto was drawing, would like to meet Sam. Having promised not to give out Sam's phone number, A. transmitted the message and Sam and Suzanne met Stravinsky the same evening. Sam told us later, in 1962, about Stravinsky's remark to him that as a composer he'd been struck by how Beckett wrote silences in *Godot*.

19

Paris, 25.5.84
Cher Avigdor

Merci de ta lettre du 19.

Ce que tu me dis de ton travail dans F.de P.*
m'intéresse et me plaît. Nous en reparlerons à Paris.
J'espère que tu auras le temps d'en juger de visu une fois
tous les éléments réunis.

Content que tu te sois remis à peindre. Je vais toujours mieux mais reste bien fatigué. Pardonne moi donc si je ne t'écris pas plus longuement.

Je vous embrasse tous – et à bientôt
Sam

* Reference to the stage design of the New York production of
Endgame for the Samuel Beckett Theater, 1984.

Paris, 25.5.84
Dear Avigdor

Thank you for your letter of the 19th.

I like and am interested in what you tell me of your
work on *Endgame*. We'll talk about it more in Paris. I
hope you have time to judge it *de visu* once all the
elements are combined.

Glad you've started painting again. I'm feeling better
but am still quite tired. Forgive me therefore if I don't
write you a longer letter.

Love to all of you – and see you soon
Sam

20

20-21 *Endgame*
The Samuel Beckett Theater, New York, 1984.
Directed by Alvin Epstein.
Set and costume design by Avigdor Arikha.
Photo © Martha Swope/ TimePix.

21

Left to right:
Alice Drummond as *Nell*
James Greene as *Nagg*
Alvin Epstein as *Hamm*
Peter Evans as *Clov*
Photo © Martha Swope/ TimePix.

Mardi

Chers amis,

terminé, je rentre.
Vu ce matin projection
du "bout à bout". Pas
mal. Reste à figurer aux
aux autres. Ça a été dur.
Je n'étonne un peu si tu es
encore à peu près solvent.
Libéralement rien fait d'autre
depuis ton arrivée. Vu personne
sauf les Reavey t fois. Horace
G. trop loin pour que je puisse
espère le voir. Je lui retéléphonerai
jeudi. et à un tas d'autres
que je n'ai pas pu voir. Une
dernière séance avec Alan pour
dresser la liste des choses à revoir.
Filming encore à préciser. Je
fais confiance à Sidney Meyers...
Type merveilleux, ex-altiste professionnel et grand amateur
de peinture. Visité au-
jourd'hui avec X Thomson Art Mus.
formidable collection. Voilà !
Je vous appellerai cette semaine.

Affectueusement

46

22

mardi, 4.08.64
Chers amis,

Terminé, je rentre. Vu ce matin projection de 'bout à bout'. Pas mal. Reste à fignoler aux autres. Ça a été dur. Je m'étonne un peu d'être encore à peu près debout. Littéralement rien fait d'autre depuis l'arrivée. Vu personne sauf les Reavey une fois. Horace G. trop loin pour que je puisse espérer le voir. Je lui téléphonerai demain, et un tas d'autres que je n'ai pas pu voir. Une dernière séance de Alan pour dresser la liste des choses à revoir. Timing encore à préciser. Je fais confiance à Sidney Meyers. Type merveilleux, ex-altiste professionnel et grand amateur de peinture. Visité aujourd'hui avec le Modern Art Mus. Formidable collection. Voilà! Je vous appellerai cette semaine.

Affectueusement
Sam

Tuesday, 4.08.64
Dear friends,

Finished. I'm coming back. This morning saw a screening from 'one end to the other'. Not bad. Finishing touches left for the others. It was rough. I'm a bit amazed that I still manage to keep on my feet. Have done literally nothing else since my arrival. Have seen no one except the Reaveys once. Horace G. too far away for me to hope to see him. I'll call him tomorrow and lots of others I couldn't see. One last meeting with Alan to draw up the list of things that need revision. Timing still to be specified. I have full confidence in Sidney Meyers. Wonderful fellow, professional ex-viola player and great amateur of art. Went together today to the Modern Art Mus. Fantastic collection. That's it! I'll call you this week.

Love
Sam

He unsurprisingly knew many musicians, like the pianists Monique Haas, Andor Foldes and, some years later, Eugene Istomin, to whom we introduced him. And the violinist Alexander (or Sasha) Schneider, of the Schneider String Quartet, was a friend through Suzanne, whom Schneider had met in Paris in the 30s and on whom, people said (it may have been Sasha himself), he had once had a crush (he told us she'd been 'a beautiful blonde'). He had known her as a pianist. Though she didn't give recitals, she and Sam played together often, until he got Dupuytren's contracture.*

Billie Whitelaw, Beckett's favourite 'instrument' – for that's how he wrote for her, and that's how she responded – tells an anecdote in her book *Who He* that bears retelling, as any playwright concerned with pacing would agree. She recalls getting a request from Beckett to 'make those three dots two dots'. Billie knew exactly what he meant. Sam also insisted on the whiteness of the tone. But the neutrality, the flatness and whiteness of the voice set against the words, did what flint does rubbed against steel: they set off a blaze.

He recited other lines as though they were tone-poems, Debussy with a brogue, so to speak; or rather, like a *Lied*, which, in fact, in later life, was the musical form to which he always returned: Schumann, Brahms and Schubert, especially Schubert's *Lieder*. To give a transcription of the way he read Apollinaire's '*La chanson du mal aimé*' I asked a musician (the harpsichordist Orhan Memed) to help me. It went something like this:

* Dupuytren's contracture is a sickening and tightening of the fibrous tissue beneath the skin on the palm of the hand. The contracture causes bending of the fourth, and frequently, the fifth finger.

23

Voie lac - tée   ô   sœur   lu – mi - neuse   Des blancs ruis - seaux   de Cha - naan

Et   des corps blancs des   a- mou - reuses   Na-geurs morts sui-vrons- nous   d' - ahan

Ton   cours   vers d'au - tres   lu - mi -neuses.

Voie lactée ô soeur lumineuse
Des blancs ruisseaux de Chanaan
Et des corps blancs des amoureuses
Nageurs morts suivrons-nous d'ahan
*Ton cours vers d'autres nébuleuses**

* 'Milky way oh gleaming sister/ From the white streams of Canaan/ And from white bodies of lovers/ Dead swimmers we'll press sorely on/ Your course towards other nebulae'

He recited a great deal from other French poets; the first time he mentioned Vincent Voiture (1598–1648), courteous in the face of my ignorance, he wrote out for me:

J'ai vécu sans nulle pensement
me laissant aller doucement
à la bonne foi naturelle
et je m'étonne fort pourquoi
la mort pense jamais à moi
*qui ne pensait jamais à elle**

* 'I lived unthinkingly/ let myself go quietly/ in good faith naturally/ and very much wonder wherefore/ death never thought of me/ who never thought of her'

There was Rabelais, and Ronsard, whom he knew very well; Racine from whom he said he'd learned so much, especially in the use of monologue as a means of revealing character; Flaubert, of course, about whom he would talk passionately, the work and the example; Verlaine, Chamfort's maxims, Rimbaud, Maurice Scève (whose '*Délie*' he gave me), Gérard de Nerval. He recommended Louise Labé; and of Mallarmé, Sam said that he had set himself, and others, a difficult task.*

* Professor Knowlson goes into these in minute detail and extensive notes in *Damned to Fame* (*op. cit.*). Therefore, I have written only of what we talked about when we three were together.

Contemporaries whom he singled out included Pierre-Jean Jouve (we talked about him after A. told Sam about meeting him again, after many years, in Sils Maria): 'a very good poet, especially before his conversion to Catholicism, a shame he recanted', but he also liked his prose, and spoke highly of *Histoires Sanglantes*; he liked Eluard (and had translated him) and the early Aragon, saying that some of the poems had real sweep in them; some of Henri Michaux as well.† Of contemporary prose writers he praised Marguerite Duras's *Le square* highly, singling it out from her later work, and Robbe-Grillet's first books, *Les gommes* and *La jalousie*; and most of all Robert Pinget, who – like so many

† He once said he'd been struck by Cocteau's use of the telephone in *La voix humaine*. (It may have unconsciously influenced his use of the tape recorder in *Krapp's Last Tape*.)

24

49

24

Paris, mardi
Cher ami,
    Merci de votre lettre.

    Je pars en Suisse demain jusqu'à la fin de la semaine.
Téléphonez moi, si vous le voulez bien, lundi prochain
le 12 vers midi.

    J'ai vu hier soir Le Square *de Marguerite Duras au*
Nouveau Théâtre de Poche, 65 rue Rochechouart. Il ne
faut pas rater ça. Ils ne peuvent pas faire de publicité et
ça va se jouer (trente fois) pour ainsi dire sans qu'on le
sache. Allez'y et dites à vos amis d'en faire autant. C'est
(pour moi) un texte infiniment émouvant et Chauffard
est très remarquable. Il faut soutenir une chose pareille.

    J'espère vous donner Krapp's Last Tape *la semaine*
prochaine. Pour le moment je n'ai que ma copie person-
nelle dont je ne peux me séparer.

    J'aurais grand plaisir à faire la connaissance de
Cuny.* Nous arrangerons ça à mon retour.

    Bien amicalement de nous deux,
    Sam

* The French actor Alain Cuny.

Paris, Tuesday
Dear friend,
    Thank you for your letter.

    I'm leaving for Switzerland tomorrow till the end of the
week. Call me, if you could, next Monday the 12th around
noon.

    I saw *Le square* by Marguerite Duras last night at the
Nouveau Théâtre de Poche, 65 rue Rochechouart. You
mustn't miss it. They can't get publicity and it'll be on
(thirty performances) without anyone knowing about it,
so to speak. Do go there and tell your friends to do the
same. It is (for me) an infinitely moving text and Chauffard is truly remarkable. Something like that must be
given support.

    I hope to be able to give you *Krapp's Last Tape* next
week. For now I only have my own copy which I can't let
go of.

    It would give me great pleasure to meet Cuny. We'll
arrange that on my return.

    With kindest regards from us both,
    Sam

others – was patently influenced by, but fought against, Beckett's style. He left Paris after this rebellion, saying about Sam *'il est vieux'* ('he's old'), and we wondered if it wasn't partly in order to find his own voice. Sam was nonplussed by his departure, especially because Pinget had been so close to Sam and Suzanne.

In later life Beckett grew impatient with the 'juvenile' literary allusions very densely embedded in his early work. Although a great reader, he disliked flaunting a too-visible wardrobe of learning; yet how could his intensive, extensive reading not enter the writing? Reading is passed down to others the way parents pass down their traits. One may even wonder if there have ever been great readers who did not go on to write in one form or another. He was an omnivorous reader. In his early work there is a great deal of wordplay, sometimes over-rife with Joycean allusions and erudition, but often hilarious; sometimes sombre, abstract – and, at times, as he himself observed, overloaded.

But one notices how gravity – in various senses – stripped back his work over time: in the sense of terrestrial gravitation as defined by physics, in the tragic, serious sense, and in the literal sense of the weight of words – fewer and fewer at the end of his life, like his preference for chamber music and *Lieder* over orchestral music. He feared erudition swamping the authenticity of a work, and constantly warned against that danger for other artists, having had to escape it himself. Sometimes, in talking to A., it was as though they were both in a war-zone, surrounded by land mines.

Once, as we three were walking down Boulevard de Port Royal and A. had been going on for nearly an hour about the theories of, variously, Vasari (Sam had given him his copy), Alberti, Cesare Ripa, Baldinucci, Lomazzo, Algarotti, Giustiniani, and others, giving dates and influences, names of benefactors and enemies, brothers and cousins and biographers by the dozen, I whispered to Sam, 'One more Italian, and I'm cutting out.' He grinned and said, 'And I'll join you.'*

* Although his respect for erudition was intense (after reading A.'s catalogue on Ingres, he wrote a letter, now lost, saying *'Chapeaux bas!'* or 'Hats off!') in spite of his reservations.

52

The same way of reciting informed Sam's approach to Shakespeare's sonnets and plays. When he came to the lines from Sonnet 71 ('No longer mourn for me when I am dead'),

> Nay, if you read this line remember not
> The hand that writ it, for I love you so...

he'd look up, and pause, letting the phrase rise like water in a fountain. The last time he recited it he told us he'd been considering writing a play around this sonnet, but gave up on the project. The lines from Sonnet 116 ('Let me not to the marriage of true minds'),

> Or bends with the remover to remove.
> O no! it is an ever-fixèd mark

made him laugh ruefully. 'Fixèd!' he would recite ironically, like a college student enjoying the enormity of the thing, of love being 'fixèd', indeed saying it *was* an enormity; but it would be completely off the mark to ascribe this to anything in his personal life (the way he recited 'For I love you so' would disprove that). He had referred to this sonnet as far back as 1932, in the last line in *Sanies II*: 'suck is not suck that alters', paraphrasing 'love is not love/ Which alters when it alteration finds'.

He – and I, when feeling confident – went through 'Since brass, nor stone, nor earth, nor boundless sea', and he loved to recite 'Shall I compare thee to a summer's day', repeating it when I stumbled over 'ow'st' in 'Nor lose possession of that fair thou ow'st'. (My faint-heartedness stemmed both from a sense of his eagle-wings hovering over the words, and from a lack of trust in my memory compared to his. Yet I had once written down – not memorized – what De Quincey, in *The Confessions of an Opium-Eater*, said: 'It is notorious that the memory strengthens as you lay burdens upon it, and becomes trustworthy as you trust it.' My memory, though I lay burdens on it, was as trustworthy as a pickpocket.) He recited from *Macbeth*, remarking on how the power of the consonants created the atmosphere, reciting the entire passage of 'Tomorrow and tomorrow and tomorrow', among others, and from *King Lear*: 'Out, vile jelly', or Lear's response to Gloucester's 'O! Let me kiss that hand!' – 'Let me wipe it first, it smells of mortality'; and Edgar's lines, especially 'The worst is not; So long as we can say, "This is the worst"' at particularly painful moments. *King Lear* was the play he could say least about, its power being indescribable as well as unstageable, perhaps because anything one could say was foredoomed to fall short. I noticed only that his face darkened, his lips tightened whenever it was mentioned. He expressed his feelings about it mostly by conveying that one couldn't.

As a rule he pronounced long or short vowels in end-rhymes without regard to their current pronunciation: 'historical rhyme' as against 'eye rhyme'. In

> Blow, blow, thou winter wind
> Thou art not so unkind...

for example, he'd pronounce 'wind' with the long i of 'unkind', as he did also in Shelley's

> O, Wind,
> If Winter comes, can Spring be far behind?

And he rhymed words ending in 'y' , as in 'silently', with 'why' if the music called for it. I also remember him defending his use of the word 'haught', in the sense of 'bearing oneself loftily', insisting delightedly that it wasn't obsolete, according to the *OED*; or his use of 'feat' in *Footfalls* – 'how feat she wheels' – about which we had some discussion: ever-conscious of that danger, too, for a writer living outside his own country and its everyday language. It is precisely the everyday 'up to his ears' or 'down on his luck' – the milk-teeth of language, too familiar to

25

be registered while one is inside the pale – that is experienced as a mixture of ache and amazement, of homesickness yet relief at being away from home, which gives a particular feeling for all languages as entailing both gain and loss. This question came up again with bruising poignance the last time he came to the house for dinner (as will be seen in the notes for '2 December or end of November 1986'*).

* See p. 122.

He was as careful with the pronunciation of rhymes in French: in his annotations to the 1916 edition of *Délie* by Maurice Scève,* for example, I found a note to the *Dizains*, CCLII, p. 175, next to the end-rhymes '*terrestres*' and '*lettres*', that said, 'This rime proves that S was not pronounced before a consonant'; or, in CCCVII, p. 210, after Scève's *vie mourante*, there's the note 'First ex.[ample] of this exp.[ression] which became very popular cf. Corneille's *Cid*,' and on p. 24, 'When Scève achieves a fine line it is an exceedingly fine line as *here*', or on p.176, on Marguerite de Navarre, 'Probably the most famous personage of 16th century. Whole Renaissance sprang from her – author of *Heptameron* – many other poems', or on p. 110, *Dizain*, CXLVIII, '*tous*' is underlined, with the remark 'Always declined in 16th cent.' (It also occasioned bringing up Daniel's *Delia*.)

* Hachette, Paris, 1916.

Not only was he careful over rhyme-endings, but equally conscious of vowel sounds, as in his annotated Petrarch (second volume of *Sonetto IX*, p. 24, in '*Le Rime, Sonetti e Canzoni*'), where '*Tanta paura e duol l'alma trista ange*' is underlined, with a note saying 'Vowels' in the margin. The same attention was paid to vowel and consonant harmonics in Yeats, Milton and Shakespeare.

Of writers or poets of the seventeenth century, besides Bunyan, whom he'd absorbed but didn't quote from much, he often recited Milton. Especially the lines 'Hail holy light' from *Paradise Lost*, Book III (with which Winnie in *Happy Days* begins Act II), recited with great but restrained emotion; the Milton music trickles like a transfusion through his work. The first evening he recited those lines, the 'h's and 'l's, placed where they were,

25

Ussy, 4.11.83

Dear Anne,

Thank you for yrs. of Oct.25 and Avigdor for his marginalis.

Happy to have good news of you all, lack of light and *Andromaque* notwithstanding.

Thank you for *feat* (adj.) examples. Few of adverbial use. My compact *OED* gives, from *The Lover's Complaint*, 'With seided sleaved silk feat and affectedly enswath'd'.

I know and like Fred Neumann. Affiliations with Mabou Mines. He has done, here and there, most recently at L.A., a discreetly dramatized *Company* of which I have had favourable accounts. He tells me he has now *Westward Ho** in his sights for similar treatment.

Here for a cure of silence & oxygen. Morning mist – afternoon sunshine.

Warrilow secured as reader for the Irish TV film. It appears he is not yet fully recovered.

Suzanne knew Sasha Schneider in the old days of the famous string quartet and greatly admired his playing. If you see him again greet him from us both. My remembrance also to Istomin.

As for me, as Bacon advised, *silemus*.[†]

Fondly to you all,

Sam

* In a rare lapse from his usual precision, Beckett means his text *Worstward Ho*.
† 'let us keep silent'.

sounded familiar, a troubling echo of other lines which I couldn't place. The next time he recited them there was the same feeling of recognition. Again I couldn't say why, but it was something in the way he recited, stopping after 'Hail', drawing out the 'hol' in 'holy'. Then, in a dream one night after an illness, I saw two parchment scrolls illuminated in black, red and gold, like medieval manuscripts, rolled out in slow motion; one entitled 'Hail holy light', the other unrolling beneath it entitled 'Hallel' (meaning 'praise' in Hebrew – hence the word 'hallelujah', 'Praise God'). 'Hallel' is a religious service consisting of a selection of psalms in Hebrew, which Milton knew well enough to translate.

There was a similarity in the alliteration and mood of exaltation, benediction and quiet ardour in that Hebrew–English encounter. The simultaneous appearance of the two scrolls was a gift from both Milton and David the psalmist – an epiphany. I recently read that Milton had the Bible read to him every morning at 4.30 a.m. in Hebrew, and that he called the Psalms 'the greatest poems in the world'.* When I thought about it, I realized that whenever Sam recited 'Hail holy light' it had sounded like a prayer.*

He talked quite often about Sterne and his daring zigzagging divagations, in the same admiring tones as when talking about Flaubert or Defoe, whose *Journal of the Plague Years* I had just read, and which he remembered being haunted by; he spoke in grave tones about the difficulties in Defoe's life and recommended Robert Louis Stevenson's letters.

He wasn't much drawn to talking about Dickens, although some passages from Dickens read like Beckett, the rhythms sometimes pulsating like his. One night, however, when he and A. were eating oysters at Les Îles Marquises, and I, having finished my salad, began quoting from *The Pickwick Papers*, which I'd just been reading – 'Wery good power o' suction, Sammy…' – he guffawed and finished the second half: 'You'd ha' made an uncommon fine oyster, Sammy, if you'd been born in that station o' life.' Dickens, like Beckett, enjoyed wordplay, but the proliferation of characters and plots in his works is totally at odds with Sam's economy. As is Balzac's. Beckett did not consider Balzac one of 'theirs', so to

* Douglas Bush, *Milton*, OUP, Oxford, 1969, p. xxiii.

* One of the earliest to remark on this was Tyndall, who, in a preface to his translation, wrote that 'The Holy Scriptures are suited particularly to English because the genius of English is like the genius of Hebrew.' (I am grateful to Professor Robert Alter for this quotation.) Trevelyan wrote, in his *History of England*, 'The effect of the continual domestic study of the book [the Bible] upon the national character, imagination and intelligence for nearly three centuries to come, was greater than that of any literary movement in our annals, or any religious movement since the coming of St Augustine. The Bible in English history may be regarded as a "Renaissance" of Hebrew literature far more widespread and more potent than even the classical Renaissance' (*History of England*, Longman, 1973, pp. 431–32.) Addison notes (in the *Spectator*, 1712, no. 405, p. 3) that 'The Hebrew idioms run into the English tongue with a particular grace and Beauty.' Poets as recent as Marianne Moore have remarked on this, too.

speak, although he'd read him well enough.* (Sam waved the subject away when I told him I was reading *Splendeurs et misères des courtisanes*, less so when *La peau de chagrin* was mentioned.) Given their radically opposed approach to economy, form and structure, I'm not sure Sam would have appreciated the comparison with Dickens.

I once told him that Horace Gregory, who had supervised my master's thesis in poetry, remembered T. S. Eliot at a party warning Auden, who was reciting some doggerel, that if he committed such inferior verse to memory, it would somehow influence his own work. Sam, who had met and liked Gregory, repeated the warning with relish, as he generally did in hearing about 'lives of the poets', but pointedly refrained from saying anything about Auden's poems, which he certainly must have read. (And with no link at all except the loose, serendipitous course fallen upon in conversation, he then went on to talk about Johnson's *Life of Richard Savage*, though it was hard to separate what Sam thought of Savage himself from his appreciation of the way Johnson championed him.)

Sam conducted his texts as though they were musical orchestrations, his actors the orchestra, as has been alluded to. Besides his incomparable reading of Clov's monologue in *Endgame* and readings from his other texts whose impact is attested to by actors who heard him run through their lines, even in translation, one of the most overwhelming was his reading of *Eh Joe*, preparatory to Billie Whitelaw's supreme interpretation. Whitelaw came to Paris for one day to rehearse it with him. Beckett had asked me to join them at the Café Français, which was near Sam's flat and ours – but why, I couldn't tell. After about an hour, I left, but during that hour Sam had read the text with several modulations, now whispering, now raising his voice, mocking, bleak. His instructions for the Voice (Billie's role), read: *'Low, distinct, remote, little colour, absolutely steady rhythm, slightly slower than normal. Between phrases a beat of one second at least,'* and so on, until, near the end, they read: '*Voice drops to whisper, almost inaudible except words in italics.*' Billie was going to stop over at our house afterwards, have a cup of tea, and rest before returning to London. When she came, my daughter Noga opened the door. Billie looked tired but exhilarated. I asked her to recite the parts they had worked on after I'd left.

What we heard – from the section 'Trailing her feet in the water like a child...' down to 'No sound...There's love for you... Compared to us...Compared to Him...*Eh Joe*?' – was a voice which no longer seemed that of a woman, but rather of waves beating against the shore, something that was part of nature, rising, falling, murmuring. We heard shingles in the shshshs, the swish of water, rocks, the pull of the tide, a rumble, Billie's arms lifting and turning as though she were thrashing in the water, ourselves on the shore, overwhelmed.

Billie was so much his instrument that he practically wrote *Not I* for her. When Sam showed him the text before it was altogether finished, A. exclaimed about the woman character, 'Her mouth is on fire,' and Sam, liking it, included that phrase in the text. We went to the opening; at one point during the performance I whispered, 'It's electrifying,' and A. said, '*C'est sidérant*'.* When we went backstage to congratulate her, Billie said, 'You'd better not touch me, I'm full of electricity.' Beckett often said *King Lear* couldn't be staged adequately. But if it were ever possible, it would certainly have to be led by such a conductor of the inexpressible.

* which means the same in French.

YEATS

In spite of his own, carefully accented way of reading poetry, it didn't seem to bother Sam that Yeats read some of his own poems, with notable exceptions (Sam had given me a tape of Yeats's readings), at breakneck speed – as though he couldn't wait to get the reading over with. Perhaps because of the tension. (One sometimes notices a similar expression on a cellist's or violinist's face, all but asking himself, 'How can I get out of here?' when playing a very difficult passage, as though balancing eggs.) He did agree that, in contrast, Dylan Thomas's readings were very good, 'memorable'. When we read Yeats's 'Sailing to Byzantium', Sam would stop at

> But such a form as Grecian goldsmiths make
> Of hammered gold and gold enamelling
> To keep a drowsy Emperor awake,

stressing the 'm' in 'form' and 'enamelling', the 'as' with a drowsy z-sound. From 1959 on, especially when we were dining at home, Yeats was as often on the menu as Samuel Johnson and Dante. Not always the same poems, though he had his favourites. Sam recited 'A Drinking Song' over a good bottle of wine, and 'The Old Men Admiring Themselves in the Water', which my daughter Alba recited with him. Another evening he'd recite the 'Girl's Song' from the 'Crazy Jane' sequence:

> I went out alone
> To sing a song or two…

When he came to the last lines –

> When everything is told,
> Saw I an old man young
> Or young man old?

– he looked up, with a glimmer in his eyes, as if to say, 'You see?' The lines from 'Why Should Not Old Men Be Mad',

> A girl that knew all Dante once
> Lived to bear children to a dunce;

were recited with indignation, anger even, as though personally offended. About 'Under Ben Bulben', he mentioned the original of the epitaph Yeats wrote as being

Hold rein. Hold breath

but that Yeats had crossed out those four words and continued directly with the final version:

Cast a cold eye
On life, on death.
Horseman, pass by!

and when I told him I preferred the first version, he disagreed, and gave examples of the *suste viator* ('halt, traveller') genre, from Swift, to Yeats's lines on Synge, and so on. This in turn led him to discuss – with immense gusto, scholar that he was, in spite of himself – the *ubi sunt* topos ('where are they now, those dead and gone'), which led inevitably to Thomas Nashe's *Summer's Last Will and Testament* in the same vein:

Brightness falls from the air
Queens have died young and fair

These lines we would end up chanting together, he stressing a pause after each line, followed by a momentary silence pregnant with feeling, sometimes followed by a predictable reference to Villon ('*Mais où sont les neiges d'antan?*'; 'But where are the snows of yesteryear?'); then both he and A. invariably proceeded to Hölderlin's *Die Titanen*, standing up in their emotion when they got to the lines:

Viele sind gestorben, Feldherrn in alter Zeit
Und schöne Frauen und Dichter
Und in neuer
Der Männer viel,
*Ich aber bin allein.**

* 'Many have died, warlords in ancient times/ And beautiful women and poets/ And in more recent many men/ I though am alone'

A. first and then Sam would linger ecstatically over the ungrammatical miracle of '*Nicht ist es aber/ Die Zeit*' ('But not is it

61

though/ Time'), *Zeit* coming where it does. Again, reciting from Yeats's 'Friends', in coming to the lines

> While up from my heart's root
> So great a sweetness flows
> I shake from head to foot,

Sam would stand up and repeat them, saying: 'Imagine such feeling – "So great a sweetness flows/ I shake from head to foot",' in amazement.

They used to stand up often, those two (I kept my seat), at certain moments of inspiration; as, for instance, in reciting the passage from Goethe (that Longfellow had translated) from *Harfenspieler*:

> *Wer nie sein Brot mit Tränen aß...*

And here too they would stand and shake their fists when they came to:

> *Der kennt euch nicht, ihr himmlischen Mächte.*

Sam did not think much of Longfellow's poems but thought
26-27   enough of his translation of Goethe's poem to write it out for me:

> Who ne'er his bread in sorrow ate,
> Who ne'er the mournful midnight hours
> Weeping upon his bed had sate
> He knows you not, ye Heavenly Powers.

26 Letter from Ussy, 31 March 1960 about a disappointing performance of *Krapp's Last Tape*.

« Freund Hain », *Er*
... ... *...*
... beaucoup à *la*
mer.

... ...
vieux. ... ...
... ... *...,*
... ... *...* *Goethe :*

« Die Welt geht auseinander
  wie ein fauler Fisch,
Wir wollen sie nicht
    balsamieren. »

Je rentre le 9 ou le
10 je ne sais pas.

...

...

Ussy, 31.3.60
Cher Avigdor,

Merci de votre lettre.

J'ai demandé à Lindon de vous faire avoir une autre invitation.[*] *J'espère que vous l'avez bien reçue.*

Suzanne est retournée voir le spectacle dimanche et hier. C.(...) est toujours aussi mauvais et le sera toujours. C'est foutu, il n'y a qu'à tirer une croix dessus. Ces cons de critiques ne comprennent rien. Plus je remâche tout ça, plus je suis désolé. Je ne travaillerai plus avec Blin.

Je n'ai pas la tête à Pim[†] *et n'ai rien fait. Ça ne m'intéresse plus et je n'y crois plus. Ça reviendra peut-être. Je passe le plus clair (!) de mon temps à regarder par la fenêtre, tantôt l'une tantôt l'autre. On ne peut même pas dire rêvasser. Je bricole un peu dehors, tire la lourde tondeuse pendant des heures, sur les mauvaises herbes.*

J'apprends par coeur Matthias Claudius! 'Freund Hain'. En être arrivé là! Pense beaucoup à la mer.

Voilà, mon pauvre vieux. C'est ce qu'il me faut en ce moment. Tombé sur les vers de Goethe:

'Die Welt geht auseinander
    Wie ein fauler Fisch,
Wir wollen sie nicht
    balsamieren.'

Je rentre le 9 ou le 10 je ne sais pas.
    Bien amicalement
    Sam

Ussy, 31.3.60
Dear Avigdor,

Thank you for your letter.

I asked Lindon to get you another invitation. I hope you got it. Suzanne went back to see the play Sunday and yesterday. C...is as bad as ever and always will be. It's screwed up, better just to forget all about it. These bloody awful critics understand nothing, The more I brood over it the sorrier I am. I won't work with Blin again.

I can't get my head round Pim and have done nothing. It no longer interests me and I don't believe in it any more. It may come back. I spend the best (!) part of my time looking out of the window, now from one, now from the other. You can't even call it daydreaming. I tinker outside a bit, pull the heavy lawnmower for hours over the weeds.

I'm learning Matthias Claudius by heart! 'Friend Death'. To get to such a point! I often think of the sea.

That's it, old chap. This is what I need right now. Found this in Goethe:

'The world is falling apart
    Like a rotten fish,
We will not
    Embalm it'

Back on the 9th or the 10th I don't know.
    As ever yours
    Sam

---

* Avigdor's invitation to the opening had been lifted by a neighbour.
† Pim is the central character in *How It Is*.

* Penultimate stanza of 'Nemt, froue, disen kranz!', pointed out in the notes to *Beckett's Collected Poems in English and French* by Federman, Fletcher, Knowlson and Calder, John Calder Publishers Ltd, 1977.

Walther von der Vogelweide was another poet whom they used to read together: Sam's poem *'Da tagte Es'*, written shortly after his father's death, refers to Walther's *'dô taget ez und muos ich wachen'*.* A. introduced Sam to the seventeenth-century poet Andreas Gryphius, whom they often read aloud, especially his *Mitternacht*, whose second line contains the phrase *'finstere Kälte bedecket das Land'* ('Dark cold mantles the land'), which A. found an echo of in Goethe's 'Prometheus': *'Bedecke deinen Himmel, Zeus'* ('Cover your sky, Zeus'). A stanza from Claudius which they recited often and which never failed to make our spines tingle came from Claudius's *'Der Tod'*:

* 'Ah, it is so dark in Death's chamber,/ Sounds so mournful when it stirs/ And then raises its heavy hammer/ And smites the hour'.

> *Ach, es ist so dunkel in des Todes Kammer,*
> *Tönt so traurig, wenn er sich bewegt*
> *Und nun aufhebt seinen schweren Hammer*
> *Und die Stunde schlägt.**

Sam presented A. with his old, small, three-volume edition of Claudius – bought during his travels in Germany – which they read out of, rather than using the edition A. had bought for himself and Sam years earlier, with notes, index, etc...Incorrigible sticklers, both of them.

On several occasions they spoke of Kafka. Sam thought his German was more *Hochdeutsch*, grown out of the Austro-Hungarian Empire rather than contemporary German. A. didn't agree and I couldn't tell the difference, but at the time Sam was reading Theodor Fontane, with its Berlin slang, which A. thinks may account for this remark. Sam also said Kafka's subject-matter called for a more disjointed style.

He would not pronounce on Rilke's poetry, except by taking exception to our enthusiasm, and declining, energetically, to hear his poems read aloud. Yet, apparently, he had liked Rilke's poem *The Song of Love and Death of the Cornet (Standard Bearer) Christoph Rilke* when he was young (which A. had illustrated as a young man) but decidedly not the *Stundenbuch* (*The Book of Hours*). Nevertheless, he never tired of reciting, along

66

with A., Goethe and his *Wandrers Nachtlied II* (also called *Ein Gleiches*), beginning, '*Über allen Gipfeln/ Ist Ruh*' ('Over all the tree-tops/ There's a hush'), one of the first poems Germans learn by heart. The fifth, seventh and eighth lines used to make us catch our breath; in fact, the poem is in a sense about the hour when one holds one's breath. He spoke of Goethe's poems in old age the way he spoke of Yeats's – as examples to read and study. Hölderlin's *Der Spaziergang* had the same effect on him, its line '*Und dann der Steg, der schmale*' ('And then the path the narrow') hinted at in *Eh Joe* in the description of 'The green one, the narrow one'. He admired Heine immensely, and the poems by Rückert set by Schubert, '*Du bist die Ruh*' and others. We remarked on how well Schubert and Schumann matched poems to their music. He also liked Trakl very much. He only once mentioned Kleist, when he saw my bilingual edition of *The Prince of Homburg* on the table – but warmly; apparently he had read a lot of him in his youth.

It should be said here that Sam did not dissect, define, analyse, deconstruct or elaborate on why he found a poem great. He had done that when a student, as his notes on Petrarch and Scève show, or later when writing about poets or novelists to clarify his thoughts, or in letters to Tom MacGreevy, his fellow Irishman and old friend from the Ecole Normale, or simply by having his characters quote or paraphrase, or by references put in obliquely. His impressions or reactions came through his body; pure spirit needed and met a body to hail and hold it, and his had been chiselled down to essentials; he'd raise a hand or look at you intensely; or lift or lower his head when repeating the lines. It was a hand lifted as in 'Ah!' or describing circles as in 'Listen to this' or 'Can you imagine?' This pact held true between the two of us for English poetry, and between him and A. – only later for me – for German poetry. Beckett had written some very pertinent, acute and acerbic criticism (about Proust and Joyce), some of it surfacing indirectly in his novels. His dumb-show, obviously, is not to be attributed to an inability to formulate the whys and hows of an oeuvre, but to great emotion underpinning and overarching his understanding of it.

This is what made him turn to Yeats so often. Yeats's 'The Tower' was particularly significant for him. He remarked on the congruence of language with visual imagery in:

> Or that of the sudden shower
> When all streams are dry,
> Or that of the hour
> When the swan must fix his eye
> Upon a fading gleam,
> Float out upon a long
> Last reach of glittering stream
> And there sing his last song.

The last four lines were recited with his head turned away as though upon a fading gleam.

After the cremation of his old friend Con Leventhal, we walked back from the cemetery (Père Lachaise, where, sitting next to us, he noted down the urn number of Con's ashes) to Con's flat, where Marion, his companion, had prepared a light buffet. Sam leaned against the wall, a glass of wine in his hand, and recited from that poem,

> Now shall I make my soul,
> Compelling it to study
> In a learned school
> Till the wreck of body,
> Slow decay of blood,
> Testy delirium
> Or dull decrepitude,
> Or what worse evil come

And here he hesitated, squared his shoulders, then went on firmly,

> The death of friends, or death
> Of every brilliant eye
> That made a catch in the breath
> Seem but the clouds of the sky...*

* Thus the title of his 1977 play...*but the clouds...*

68

He would recite from 'At the Hawk's Well', and talk of Yeats's
last poems of and in old age. Along with the catalogues he gave
me of Yeats's exhibitions, both of the poet and his brother, the
painter (he owned two paintings by Jack Yeats), he gave me the
correspondence between Yeats and Dorothy Wellesley. He avoided a direct answer when I asked what he thought of Dorothy
Wellesley, but he'd kept the book all those years, merely saying he thought it would interest me. Each time he came back to
Yeats's last poems, and each time would urge me to read them
again. A standard of comparison. He himself wrote poems on
old age, as in

Age is when to a man
huddled o'er the ingle
Shivering for the hag
To put the pan in the bed
And bring the toddy
She comes in the ashes
Who loved could not be won
Or won not loved
Or some other trouble
Comes in the ashes
Like in that old light
The face in the ashes
That old starlight
On the earth again.*

* From 'Words and Music', in *Cascando and Other Short Pieces*, Grove Press, New York, 1963, p. 23.

There was a curious and somewhat painful incident involving literary allusions – who remembered what – which had rankled in
Con (his friend since Trinity College days) for about forty years.
A. first met Con and his wife Ethna (Sam's old flame) in 1958
when he travelled to Dublin, with letters of introduction to all
of Sam's old friends and teachers at Trinity College. A., Con and
Ethna met every day of his sometimes sober stay there, went to the
races, talked in pubs. Just before Con's imminent move to Paris,
Sam wanted to give me a notion of Con's humour, to let me know

how knowledgeable a man Con was, how quick and witty. He told the following story: 'One night Con and I were strolling slowly in Dublin, along the Liffey and we saw a young couple embracing. Immediately Con quipped, "Night's Young Thoughts".' Sam relished the reference to Young's 'Night Thoughts'. Con had known many poets, such as MacNeice and others of his generation, and had been active in the Abbey Theatre. (And had offered to read my poems at a reading organized by Patrick Bowles in the old American Centre in Paris.)

Nearly twenty years later, on one of the last evenings A. and I spent with Con before he died, holding on to his never-empty glass of wine (he once admitted that he never really drank, just sipped), he told us, 'Oh, you know, Sam wasn't always a saint. One night we saw a couple embracing and I said, "Night's Young Thoughts". Sam liked it, all right, liked it so much I think he quoted it as one of his own inventions.' No matter how much I insisted to the contrary, telling him how Sam had appreciated his *esprit*, that in fact it was the first thing I knew about Con before even meeting him, he wasn't convinced, and after forty years was still smarting.

Despite this supposed theft, needless to say Sam and Con remained staunch, loyal, loving confidants till the end. And of course I never mentioned it to Sam.

Sam would quote from Keats; loved 'full-throated ease', 'To take into the air my quiet breath' and 'While thou art pouring forth thy soul abroad' (from *Ode to a Nightingale*); agreed that Shelley's 'Pourest thy full heart/ In profuse strains of unpremeditated art' enacted a similar ecstasy of birdsong, but, while admiring it, would come back to Keats's 'full-throated ease' and the Letters. We didn't talk about or read from the Letters until the 1970s, when I first read them. I mentioned the 'Negative Capability' passage to Sam, who of course had read it when he studied Keats; when I came to 'when a man is capable of being in uncertainties, mysteries, doubts, without any irritable reaching after fact and reason' he became tense with attention, suddenly sitting bolt upright as

28 Dinner in the studio, c.1981
Left to right: Alba, Noga, Anne and Sam.

though pierced by an electric current, and asked me to read it again at the table, and repeated excitedly, 'irritable reaching after fact and reason – that's it, capable of being in uncertainties'. He didn't have to explain why he found this so important; the link to his own work was so obvious.

28

THE BIBLE

Beckett had several editions of the Bible – four in different languages (the *Family Bible, la Sainte Bible, L'Antico Testamento,* the Luther Bible) – as well as at least one concordance and the *Book of Common Prayer.* His mother had been a Quaker, and Bible-reading was important. As a Protestant, he'd read the Old Testament as well as the New. We used to read the Psalms together, he and I taking turns with the King James version, A. reading, or reciting by heart, the Hebrew. His indirect references to Job in his work are also discernible. Because English resonates with Hebrew and biblical cadence, Beckett translates very easily into Hebrew, and in fact biblical structures and references, however disguised, are sprinkled throughout his texts, which is of course true, almost inescapably so, for many writers and poets. Thus the use of the cohortative in *Lessness*: 'He will curse God again as in the blessed days ' or 'He will stir in the sand...He will live again the space of a step'; 'It will be day and night again over him the endlessness the air heart will beat again,' which resonates with lines in the Psalms and the Prophets: 'Our God shall come, and shall not keep silence'; 'I shall not die, but live…and I will declare thy greatness…I will extol thee, my God, O king', inverted in *Lessness* into 'calm long last all gone from mind. He will curse God again as in the blessed days.'

Moreover, Beckett invents words by compression, like the word 'lessness' itself, which qualifies as correct and syntactical in Hebrew. The French poet Yves Bonnefoy suggested, in a conversation about Bible translation, that English and German poetry (although German is more modular) differ so much from French poetry because the English and German Bibles were inspired translations, and translated from or based on the Hebrew, whereas the French translation is based on the Latin, and has mostly Latin resonances; and, although Bonnefoy didn't add this, has the more formal structure and rhythms of a prayer book.

As an instance of Beckett's acute intuition of languages which he hadn't even studied, in this case Hebrew, there are two episodes which stand out, one concerning *Krapp's Last Tape* which took place before I arrived in Paris, and the other *Godot*: Sam had given the *Krapp's Last Tape* typescript to A. in 1958 for the Hebrew quarterly *Qeshett* no. 1 (with which A. was originally involved) for publication even before its appearance in the *Evergreen Review*.* The editor, Aharon Amir, had translated it, and sent the translation for approval to A., who corrected it with Sam. Listening to it line by line in Hebrew, Sam tapped his finger on the desk whenever he felt that something was wrong. 'Too many syllables.' 'Too long.' 'Not the right rhythm.' He was always spot on.

Similarly in 1965, when A. was sent the Hebrew translation of *Godot* by another writer, Moshé Shamir, and which he rewrote for two weeks before showing it to Sam. This time I was present, as occasional arbiter, while they worked. A., to be fair, first read Shamir's version, then his own: Sam unerringly stopped A. at

* Though *Qeshett* published it in its fall issue whereas *Evergreen* published it in the summer.

72

the same point A. had queried the translation, when he felt the Hebrew jarring with the original, and corroborated the second version with a tap.

From the New Testament, Sam's favourite Gospel was Luke, although one finds Mark and others in his work. (And it appears from Dr David Flusser's new work that, of the four Gospels, Luke's portrayal of Jesus most closely preserves the *Ur*-text, which again corroborates Sam's intuition.)* He would recite the parable from Luke 12, reading the lines about the rich man with sarcasm, then thundering, 'Thou fool, this night thy soul will be required of thee', looking as stern as a prophet. From the Old Testament, A. would read the chapters on Elijah rebuking Ahab for coveting Naboth's vineyard, and then Nathan's denouncement of David's behaviour; once or twice he read the first chapters of Samuel in Hebrew, which Sam seemed to be familiar with from the rhythms of the King James version. He enjoyed hearing A. read Chapter 4 of Jonah in Hebrew. When God asks Jonah, after the worm 'smote the gourd that it withered', whether he wishes himself to die, Jonah says, in the King James version, 'I do well to be angry, even unto death,' the more idiomatic translation being, 'I've had it!' Or '*J'en ai marre*', in French. He often said he wondered what it was that Jesus was writing in the dust. The personality and example of Jesus is referred to throughout Sam's oeuvre.

Mocking his own supposed laziness, Sam would say, 'Go to the ant, thou sluggard,' but whereas most people remember only that part, he'd quote to the end of the line: 'Consider her ways and be wise.' (The same was true for Bishop George Berkeley's 'Westward the course of empire...' which he'd quote to the end.) He also quoted the lines about the two thieves from St Augustine ('Do not despair: one of the thieves was saved, do not presume: one of the thieves was damned'), which would lead in turn to a few lines from Ecclesiastes. We would discuss parallels and differences between Jewish and Christian sources. His feeling for these sources had everything to do with being a writer and the truth he demanded of a sentence, and little to do with religious belief.

* David Flusser, *Jesus*, The Magnes Press, Jerusalem, 1997.

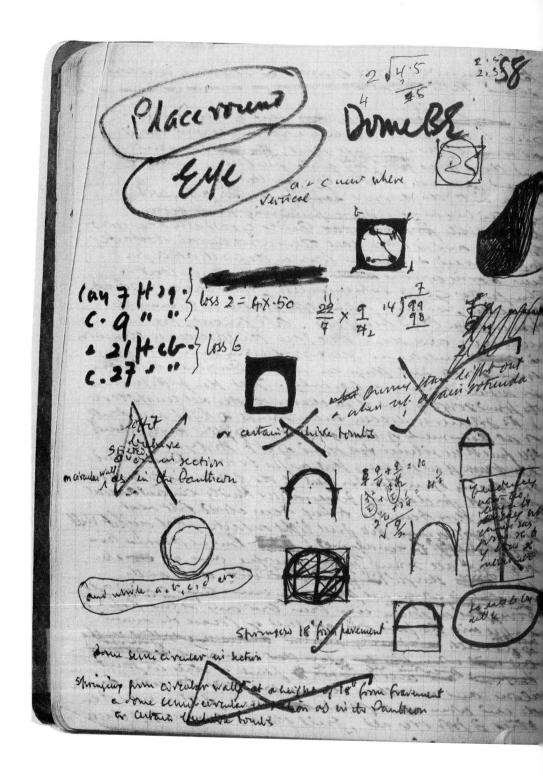

29 Two pages from the 93pp manuscript of *Imagination Dead Imagine*,
17 August 1964–19 March 1965.

an angle a and the rest the only way, line such hair over ... clear or ... or ...
... you to ... box ... ... view,
the hair so clear when ... on face is gone
for the moment, ... it for the moment ...
I come back to one another view and in the
face and ... all the glare for the moment.
... ... cheek brow ...
... ... for ... ... long black lashes
in the vivid white cheek line so clear ... ...
... gay in hair before ... all turned back and lost
for some reason and face quite ...
... ... the earth ... ...
... it self ... with ... two lashes ex-
... to say the least ... ...
... and so you will ... a ... other classes ...
quite gone. Clear here to ... from the face to
note how place no longer ... but ... a ...
rotunda ... circular ... ...
... eighteen inches in height ... a ...
semicircular in ... as in the ... as there
... ... and consequently there
feet from pavement to ... ... is at its highest
point no lower than before with ... of floor
space in the ... of ... per or
... square inches per ... ... a will.
... for ... readily acquired
and ... on ... ... of little
... for the moment, ...
... ...
... ...
... a, b, c, d now when any
pair of right angles dividers met ...
... ... for ... ...
nearly one foot for ... head to arm and of ...
more than one foot for arm to knees and of
nearly one foot for knees to feet ...
... be over seven foot tall ...
... correct filling is a ... ...
... in such a way that if head left
check at a and feet at c then are no longer
at new d but ... somewhere between it

Though sometimes we wondered. The Irish seem to have a tender way with God. Sam kept the Irish 'God bless' for good-byes and 'Please God' for well wishes. In *Godot* there are also several instances: for example, to Vladimir's protests that Estragon can't compare himself with Christ, Estragon replies, 'All my life I've compared myself to him.' In bringing up paradigmatic figures in the Old Testament, we talked about Abraham and Moses, the qualities of mercy and compassion, the Hebrew root of 'compassion', *rahamim*, being the same as for 'womb', *rehem*. He was extremely struck by the story of the rabbis who, in discussing the end of time, say justice will be absolute, and one of them, Rav Ulla, adding, 'May I never see that day' (Babylonian Talmud, Sanhedrin, 68.) Chuckle of agreement. It sounded like something he might have said.

JOHNSON

Johnson was the one subject most certain to animate Sam, no matter how despondent he'd been before. There were many evenings, as mentioned, when he could say nothing, show nothing, would hide his eyes and answer mechanically, albeit with his never-failing courtesy, until Johnson's name came up (I'd bring it out like whiskey, or medicine). He dipped into Johnson constantly, for sheer pleasure; it was a source of relief, and, for the sake of our conversations, he was very glad that I considered it such, too. My considering Austen a 'relief', on the other hand, and a great novelist, he absolutely disagreed with, even after I reminded him what Sir Walter Scott had written about his 'Big Bow-Wow Strain' as compared with Austen's style.*

He had held a very different view of Austen when he was younger, as I discovered only after reading Knowlson's biography, which quotes opinions expressed in Sam's letters to Tom MacGreevy. He had even taken his mother to see Austen's house, and referred to her as the 'divine Jane':[†] 'She had much to teach me.' Sam never alluded to his earlier opinion. Wondering what it was about Austen that he could no longer

* Written 14 March 1826: 'Also read again and for the third time at least Miss Austen's very finely written novel of *Pride and Prejudice*. That young lady had a talent for describing the involvements and feelings and characters of ordinary life which is to me one of the most wonderful I ever met with. The Big Bow-Wow Strain I can do myself like any now going but the exquisite touch, etc...' (*The Journal of Sir Walter Scott*, Canongate Classics, Edinburgh, 1998). About fifty years earlier Boswell had quoted Lord Pembroke as saying, 'Dr Johnson's sayings would not appear so extraordinary were it not for his bow-wow way' (Boswell's *The Life of Samuel Johnson*, entry for 27 March 1775).

† Knowlson, *op.cit.*, p. 742, note 26.

accept, some possibilities came to mind; perhaps that in Austen virtue and decency are in a sense rewarded, sometimes materially, sometimes only by the approval of the beholder. Vulgarity and insensitivity are punished, chastised, though both virtue and vice still have to sustain her fine sense of ridicule. The world closes in neatly, but sometimes oppressively. The deep unhappiness and helplessness of some of her heroines lend themselves to some sort of resolution (and later, in Woolf, they'd have a room of their own without depending on a husband or anyone else). Although of a different order, was Austen's spirit, like Bach's, too steeped in the certainties of another age, from Sam's point of view? Because, for Sam, language was the only possibility of leaving a true trace of 'How it is', though for him, too, humour afforded relief. His own rectitude, like a wick going through his spine, would merely find the term 'reward' repellent.

He had innumerable books concerning Johnson, as well as a 1799 edition of his *Dictionary*. One day he came in with a delighted expression on his face, giving a quick rub to his nose, smoking his cigar, saying, 'Just read this in Johnson's *Dictionary* – his definition of "lamentation": "audible wail".' He had even written a play about him which he regarded as juvenilia. Johnson's conversation – in spite of his notorious rages – was for Sam the paradigm of civilization and proportion; his kindness and hospitality to the poor and helpless, exemplary. Lord Chesterfield's conduct as described in Johnson's 'Letter to a Noble Lord' filled him with indignation – he'd recite parts of it ('Is not a patron, my Lord...') from memory; Johnson's not liking 'to come down to vacuity' made him grin, the virtues and problems of Mrs Thrale he sympathized with, and so on. We took turns in remembering favourite passages, I mainly in paraphrase, and he, of course, by heart. When I read to him Boswell's report, in 1770, of Johnson's remarks on Burton's *Anatomy of Melancholy* – 'the only book that took him [Johnson] out of bed two hours sooner than he wished to rise' – Sam brought me his beautiful three-volume edition of Burton the next time he came.

In the latter part of his life he wanted to get rid of as many books as possible – not Dante, of course, of which he had many editions (except one which he gave to Noga in 1988, a beautiful edition he'd forgotten A. had presented to him some thirty years earlier), nor Johnson's *Dictionary* (although again he did present Noga with *The Poetical Works of Samuel Johnson 1785*). He gave me George Moore's three-volume *Hail and Farewell*, which described scenes, landscapes and people probably very familiar to him (he also mentioned Moore's *Esther Waters*). We sometimes exchanged books we'd read (one he liked very much was David Arkell's *Looking for Laforgue* which Istomin had given me); we talked a lot about Laforgue and how often he mentioned the rue Berthollet, where he lived, near to both our flats. Sam and I each went separately to look at No. 5, with the blue door he was so moved by. I tried to interest the committees at the town hall to put up a plaque commemorating Laforgue's stay there, but could not get their permission.

Sam never asked to keep any book I lent him, not even Saul Bellow's *Herzog*, which he found excellent, nor most of those A. lent him, however interesting he found them – as, for example, the life of Loyola by Ludwig Marcuse. He liked other American writers, once asking me if I'd read Malcolm Lowry who, though English, had written three novels in the United States (*Under the Volcano* being the one he mentioned particularly), and other playwrights, Americans such as Edward Albee and Israel Horowitz, but we did not discuss them as much as English writers. But there was one he did want to keep: on a one-week trip to New York in the fall of 1988 I had come across the relatively recent biography of Johnson by Walter Jackson Bate, and didn't leave my room for three days as a result, so engrossed was I. On my return I told Sam about it (by then he was in the old-age home, Le Tiers Temps). He was a bit sceptical, saying he'd read everything, from Boswell onwards: Hester Lynch Piozzi, Hawkins, etc...I pressed this book on him, knowing there was material in there which he couldn't possibly have read. I did not have to wait long for his reaction. For the first and only time he asked whether he could keep it, looking at me very intently, his eyes all but declaring, 'No way, sorry, you can't say no.'

We talked about it at subsequent meetings, going over favourite titbits: Johnson's miserable time in Oxford, his shame at not having the proper shoes; the time that – as I kept reminding him – Oliver Edwards, one of Johnson's fellow students, said, on meeting him again, 'You are a philosopher, Dr Johnson. I have tried too in my time to be a philosopher but I don't know how, cheerfulness was always breaking in.' Or the extraordinary George Psalm-anazar, etc...Sam often spoke of those in any way connected to Johnson or his period – 'Kit' Smart ('I'd as lief pray with Kit Smart as anyone else') and his circle of friends, Garrick, Burney, Goldsmith, etc. – as though he'd known them intimately. He did.

DANTE

If Johnson was his interlocutor, Dante was his mentor. As mentioned above, he had several editions, and he always came back to and gravely commended the Cary translation to me. There are quotations from and references and allusions to Dante throughout Beckett's work, early and late. As a young man in Florence he apparently always carried a small copy of Dante. (In connection with the *Inferno* and *Purgatorio* he often spoke of his Italian teacher, Bianca Esposito, and of his stay with her family, whom he loved, outside Fiesole, when he was twenty-one.)

Some time in 1968, he quoted a passage which I couldn't write down fast enough, and so the next time he patiently dictated it again – with the same patience and courtesy with which he dictated Voiture's poem mentioned earlier – a long passage from Boccaccio's lecture on Dante's dream about the peacock. He outlined, from memory, the main quotes from Boccaccio's lecture, which are a justification of the structure and language of *The Divine Comedy*, with a peacock as the central allegory. (He told me at the time where he'd first read it, but I didn't copy down the source.)

I The peacock's hundred eyes, or feathers, or plumage = the hundred chants of *The Divine Comedy*: 3 x 33 + 1. *The Prologue* and *Inferno* consist of 34 chants. *Purgatorio* of 33. *Paradiso* of 33.*

* Dante's influence on Beckett's use of mathematics can be surmised here. Beckett was good at mathematics and enjoyed using them for attacking problems of choreography and dialogue in plays and novels, as has been mentioned earlier.

II The peacock's harsh voice corresponds to Dante's voice chastising sinners.

III Contrasting with the beautiful plumage are the ugly feet, corresponding to the ugly Vulgate tongue Dante is using.

IV The peacock's incorruptible flesh corresponds to the sweet odour of incorruptible verity.

In his cracked voice there was an urgency like that of a Credo, which remains with me to this day, when he came to the 'sweet odour of incorruptible verity'.

He quoted extensively from the *Inferno* and some of Joyce's remarks on it. From *Purgatory*, Canto 13, 89, he recited –

Sì che chiaro
*Per essa scenda della mente il fiume.**

– and recalled Joyce's remarks on the word *fiume* sounding regret for the past.

The very first year I met him, 1959, I remember him quoting Petrarch's *'chi può dir com' egli arde, è 'n picciol foco'* as being of special significance to him. He had quoted it too to A. in the early 1950s. I hadn't yet studied Italian, let alone Petrarch's Italian, so he translated this line: 'He who knows he is burning is burning in a small fire.' He sent A. the reference on a card. It was from the *In Vita di M. Laura* sequence, Sonnet CXVIII, beginning *'Più volte già dal bel sembiante umano.'* The last tercet reads:

E veggi' or ben, che caritate accesa
Lega la lingua altrui, gli spirti invola.
*Chi può dir com' egli arde, è 'n picciol foco.**

An unidentified 1919 translation, has: 'Ah! Now I find that fondness to excess/ Fetters the tongue, and overpowers intent./ Faint is the flame that language can express.'

* 'That the stream of memory may flow down through it clear'; translated by Charles Eliot Norton, *Encyclopaedia Britannica*, London, 1952.

* It is only recently, in rereading Montaigne's *Les Essais* (Arica, 1992) that I found the same line quoted, in Chapter II, but in the context of lovers who want to represent an unbearable passion. For Beckett, the same quotation probably comprehended all unbearable passions.

30

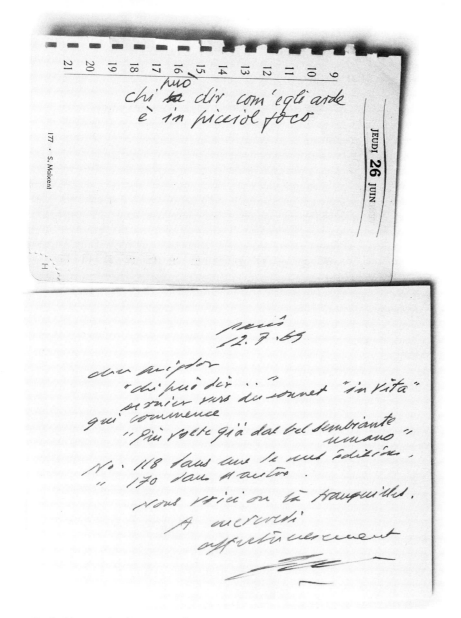

chi può dir com'egli arde
è in picciol foco

177 · S. Maixent

Paris
12. 7. 65

cher ami ador
«chi può dir ...»
dernier vers du sonnet "in vita"
qui commence
"Più volte già dal bel sembiante
umano"
No. 118 dans une de mes éditions.
" 170 dans d'autres.
nous voici en la tranquillité.
A mercredi
affectueusement

30   Card with quotation from Petrarch.

81

SONETTO IX

NON HA PIÙ SPERANZA DI RIVEDERLA , E PERÒ SI
CONFORTA COLL'IMMAGINARSELA IN CIELO.

S'Amor novo consiglio non n' apporta,
    Per forza converrà, che 'l viver cange:
    Tanta paura e duol l'alma trista ange,
    Che 'l desir vive, e la speranza è morta:

Onde si sbigottisce, e si sconforta
    Mia vita in tutto; e notte e giorno piange,
    Stanca, senza governo, in mar, che frange,
    E 'n dubbia via senza fidata scorta.

Immaginata guida la conduce;
    Che la vera è sotterra, anzi è nel Cielo,
    Onde più che mai chiara al cor traluce,

Agli occhi no; ch' un doloroso velo
    Contende lor la desïata luce,
    E me fa sì per tempo cangiar pelo.

Vowels

31 A page from Beckett's copy
of *Le Rime di Messer Francesco
Petrarca*

This quotation from Petrarch we found in the two-volume set, *Le Rime di Messer Francesco Petrarca* (from the Classica Biblioteca Italiana series), which he'd bought when he was twenty and gave A. much later. What A. and I found significant was that the line he quoted was in the *un*annotated volume, the first, whereas he'd heavily annotated the second. Obviously the sonnet had burned into his memory without his having had to look it up. In effect, it was close in connotation to that other line he quoted as often, from the beginning of our friendship till the end of his life, Edgar's 'The worst is not; So long as we can say, "this is the worst."' Jocelyn Herbert remembers Sam writing that line to her in her bereavement, after her life-long companion George Devine died.

Implied here is his stoic attitude to life, to that which must be endured, life not to be tampered with – his love of Leopardi, Schopenhauer, his appreciation of Cioran, and deeply felt sense of the tragic and the hopeless notwithstanding; or rather, not contradicting his stance. 'The Dialogue between Plotinus and Porphyry' in the *Operette Morali* of his beloved Leopardi (though we never talked about this particular work) expresses much of his own point of view in its irony, disenchantment and contained despair. It ends with Plotinus having the last word – that one must endure: 'Let us not refuse to bear that part of the ills of our species destiny has assigned us.'*

* *Operette Morali, Essays and Dialogues, Giacomo Leopardi*, University of California Press, Berkeley, p. 477.

An accomplished and enthusiastic sportsman (he'd try not to accept invitations when the rugby internationals were on, on Saturday afternoons), and by all accounts in his youth a great cricketer, swimmer and walker, Sam possessed what sportsmen seem to have in common, which is precisely the ability to endure: 'I can't go on I must go on I go on.' His comments to A. on Giacometti's theory of failure, close to but essentially different from his own, was '*l'échec à récupération*' – recuperated failure, with which he couldn't agree. The lines from Petrarch and from Edgar in *King Lear* were on the contrary like a (doomed) battle-cry.

He was always prompt in obliging me with quotations and translations, especially from the Latin. He seemed to enjoy the

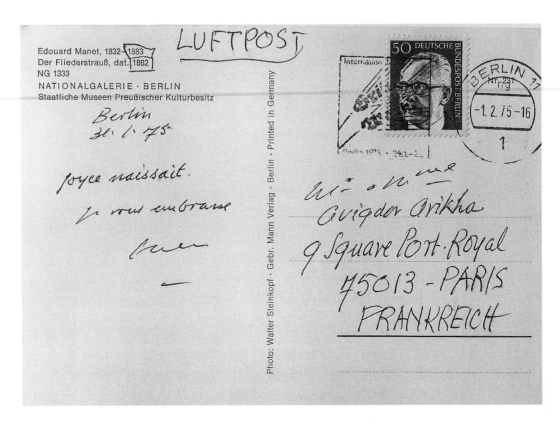

32 Joyce was born.

challenge of it, of refreshing his own knowledge of it. I'd never have bothered him with the common Latin expressions or tags listed in dictionaries, but when I came across a long passage I turned to him. He'd copy it down on a piece of paper, work on it a while at home, and send me the result by mail.

He spoke to us and to a few others about his relations with Joyce and Joyce's children. (We got a card dated 31 January 1975 saying:

32 *'Joyce naissait'*, 'Joyce was born'.)

Whenever we dined at Le Mont Blanc, a restaurant near rue Casimir Perrier, Sam would remember Paul Léon, who used to live near by (we sometimes met Henri Michaux who also used to frequent this restaurant). Léon had been an important member of the Resistance cell which Sam later joined. He would talk about the pleasant evenings spent in the Léon household, with sadness in his voice because of Léon's arrest, internment near Paris and subsequent death in the camps, and would speak of

84

Léon's part in the translation of *Finnegans Wake*, the Anna Livia Plurabelle section especially. Sam rarely spoke of his own actions in the Resistance. Apart from infrequent references made to several of his friends, it was an imperfectly known chapter in his life prior to Knowlson's assiduous researches. (Some time in the 1950s Gabrielle Buffet-Picabia, who distinguished herself during the war by her heroism, and who was in the same cell as Sam and Suzanne, told A. the details of their role, and of their escape from Paris to the south of France, details which Sam confirmed.) Was it because he felt embarrassed in front of A., who had been in a concentration camp? Or because of his modesty?

Others have written in detail about the relationship between Beckett and Joyce, but there is one anecdote which Sam recounted to A., which I don't think has appeared elsewhere. It took place, Sam told him, when René Crevel came to present the second Surrealist Manifesto to Joyce, as an oblique inducement to him to join the group. Peering closely at the text, after a long silence Joyce asked him: *'Pouvez vous justifier chaque mot?'* Silence. Then, *'Car moi, je peux justifier chaque syllabe.'* ('Can you justify every word? Because I can justify every syllable.')

An unfamiliar poem, which Sam recited at home in about 1960, contained the lines that Swift wrote with Tom Sheridan (*he* called him Tom):

All devouring, all destroying
Never tired, never cloying
Never finding full repast
Till it eats the world at last.

He often recited Swift's famous epitaph, and said of him that he was in a cage, meaning Ireland. In a lighter mood, John Gay's epitaph once came to mind:

Life is a jest and all things show it.
I thought so once and now I know it.

When we once talked of Housman he recalled the lines from 'When I watch the living meet':

And the bridegroom all night through
Never turns him to the bride,

finding them very funny – 'they both really should be on better terms' (that the bride and groom were both dead did not make the image any less awkward). He often referred to Jeremy Taylor's *Holy Dying* very respectfully, warmly even, as well as to Sir Thomas Browne's *Urn Burial*, both of which, at his urging, I began to read. I could not get through the first, to his surprise and mild disappointment, though I found *Urn Burial* and *Religio Medici* more accessible and relevant, and so he'd refer to those instead. Donne he referred to, but did not recite, once speaking of the *Elegies* but remaining silent when I mentioned 'Death be not proud'. He often spoke of Sr Juana Inés de la Cruz, whom he had translated with Octavio Paz; and of Racine and verse-plays in general.

The following passage found in Sam's Berlin notes written in January 1937 bears very much on what Sam said to us one night about T. S. Eliot's plays. After a performance of Hebbel's tragedy *Gyges und sein Ring*, Sam wrote that he had seen enough to convince him that 'the poetical play can never come off as play, nor when played as poetry either, because the words obscure the action and are obscured by it...the play is such good poetry that it never comes alive at all...Racine never elaborates the expression in this sense, never stands by the word in this sense, and therefore his plays are not "poetical", undramatic, in this sense.'* After reading this, his remarks to us about T. S. Eliot as dramatist (see below) and about the poetry and 'unstageability' of *King Lear* appear consistent with his own work. But poetry, integral to Beckett's plays, does not lessen the dramatic impact but, rather, heightens it.

He liked to recite, in unison, Sir Walter Raleigh's 'Even such is Time...' (since he loved to share the lines he loved, as has been

* Knowlson, *op.cit.*, p. 246. Even someone as different from Beckett as Sir Walter Scott said that 'perhaps a play to act well should not be too poetical' (Sir Walter Scott, *The Journal*, Edinburgh, 1998, p. 339).

SAMUEL BECKETT

Dear Anne

"No gardener has died within rosaceous memory." The conceit is in Fontenelle, Entretiens sur la Pluralité des mondes.

"De mémoire de rose on n'a vu que le même jardinier." F. lasted on to 100 (1657-1757).

love to you all

sam

33 Beckett's translation for Fontenelle's *'mémoire de rose'*.

shown), just as he wrote out for us his own beautiful translation of Fontenelle, from *Entretiens sur la Pluralité des mondes*: '*De mémoire de rose on n'a vu que le même jardinier*' – 'No gardener has died within rosaceous memory.'

33

He also translated Rimbaud, Breton, Eluard, Crevel; and often talked of Gérard de Nerval, Joachim du Bellay, Chateaubriand (chiefly his *René*), Montale, Leopardi – the last always calling up Schopenhauer in his wake, an extremely and understandably important figure in Sam's life – and other Italian and Spanish poets. There were times when listening to him was like attending the courses he'd taken at Trinity College with his professors Thomas Rudmose-Brown, R. B. D. French (whom A. had met in Dublin in 1958) and H. O. White, whose knowledge had been given wings by a poet, one affectionate and ever grateful to them. What follows is an exact rendition of the notes taken then with some lines left out. Explanations are in brackets.

October 1970 After the cataract operation on the 14th: The clinic is a short walk from our house, on Boulevard Arago, Clinique de Sainte Marie de la Famille. Leaves already thick on the ground, early October. S. loved to shuffle his feet through them; told us each autumn how, as a young boy, would do just that with his father. Clinic is an old house, a kind of convent, dark brown wooden stairs, doors creaking, thick, like a Van der Weyden. A nun passes, white bonnet, wimple, triangular face, eyes lowered. Sam's room called 'Sainte Marguerite'. We knock at the arranged time exactly, he opens the door, in wine-coloured pyjamas, left eye bandaged, crack in voice, kiss. Murmurs of gladness. Back into bed. Fruit on mantelpiece. More like an English room in an old mansion. High ceiling, brass bed-stand, view of garden from window, several chairs. We draw near. Tells us how it went, a note of exhilaration. 'Anaesthesia? Felt nothing, *un délice, c'était un délice*' ('a delight, it was a delight') but when bandage removed, for one moment *une terrible clarté* ('a terrible clarity'). A small radio on his bed demonstrates it – switches on; 'France Musique. Brahms'. Switches off and on a few times to show how well he can do it – then off, now is not the time for music. We are perhaps some of his first visitors. What does he do since he can't read? '*Je me dis* ['I recite'] *des poèmes.*' We leave it at that. We tell him about the telegrams and enquiries after his health. He describes the doctor: '*un type très bien; manière très sèche. Sept enfants. Petite taille – presque chauve. Très bien.*'* Sentences chiselled as in his work. I then ask – what kind of poems – which ones? Goethe. Recites *Prometheus*. All seven stanzas. Then from Verlaine. Says of him, '*Mais quel déchet!*' ('What a waste!') Wrote so much, Verlaine. Not Goethe? 'Of course.' In the *Prometheus* he comes to the line, '*...unter der Sonne als euch, Götter!*' ('Under the sun like you, Gods!'). What beautiful emphasis. Grave irony. Challenging, stern, reproof. More Goethe. Other poems. Light falls. Gets tired.

[In August 1974, Edward played with the New Irish Chamber Orchestra in the chapel at the Sorbonne. I went alone, and met

* 'A very good sort; very dry manner. Seven children. Small – nearly bald. Very good.'

34 *Samuel Beckett, Double Profile,*
5 February 1971.
Gold-point on bluish coated paper
26 x 21 cm.

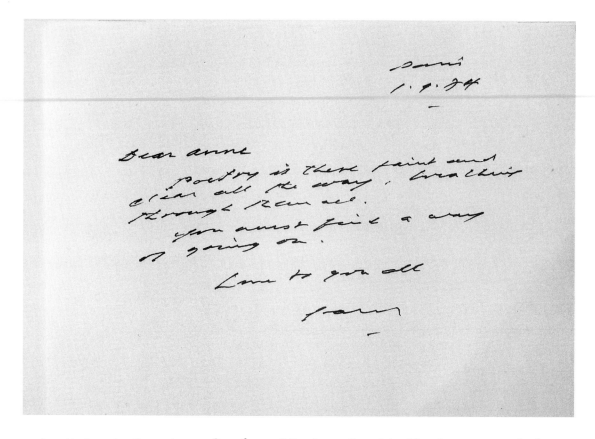

35 A card to Anne about her work.

Sam there, sitting in another aisle. After the concert we both went up to congratulate Edward. There was another young musician standing near him, who, after Sam had said how much he'd liked the playing, adding, 'Bravissimo', asked Sam his name, and got the answer, Samuel Beckett. The musician asked him affably, 'And what do you do, are you a musician, too?' Sam answered, not at all taken aback, 'Oh, no. I just like music.' (Beckett had received the Nobel Prize in 1969.)

35   In that same year he sent me a card, after a particularly discouraging period in my work. 'Poetry is there faint and clear all the way, breathing through them all. You must find a way of going on.' It sounded as though it were gasping.

10 October 1974 Dinner. About the fruit on the table I said it reminded me of Caravaggio, he said Cornelis de Heem. A. spoke about Manet and his amputation, his end in Bellevue, and Sam cited Manet's painting *La route des gardes*. We spoke of Israel, history. After coffee, we talked about T. S. Eliot, *The Wasteland* [*sic*], the *Four Quartets*, S. said that he found Eliot too deliberate. But that some of his poems were written with fire. Also true of *Murder in the Cathedral*, but he wasn't really a dramatist. But wondered how Eliot could ever have allowed another man to change his work. Wouldn't hear of Ezra Pound, who had been very rude to him when he was young. Spoke of his own translation of Rimbaud's *Bateau ivre*, given to an Irish friend who, years later, had rescued it from a flaming house as one of the precious objects; heard about it in the mail that very morning from Knowlson of Reading University. Spoke of English *qua* English. Then, 'Poetry. That intractable beast. An untamed horse. A wild animal one has to ride.' Reminded me of Virginia Woolf's image in *The Waves* (he never wanted to talk about Woolf, no matter how often I brought her up): 'Words and words and words, how they gallop, how they lash their long manes and tails' etc...but I didn't show it to him then. Begins to recite from Yeats's 'At the Hawk's Well': 'I call to the eye of the mind...' down to 'The salt sea wind has swept bare.' Recited Apollinaire, like a chant: '*Voie lactée*'.

Friday, 21 March 1975 Brought us beautiful edition of *Pas moi*, and catalogue of Jack Yeats. Talked about Berlin; about the actor who, appalled at the enormity of the part, produced a medical certificate, and quit, though everyone's schedule for rehearsals pivoted around his free time. Restaurants were empty, ate sometimes at the Giraffe, where he was the only customer. Brought A. the oil colours he'd asked for, nearly 25 tubes. Loved the names *Caput mortuum* and *Deckweiss*. While I rolled out the still half-folded trolley just before dinner, I saw him standing against the closed door of the children's play-room. So quiet and intense his standing, I thought he was stricken with sadness, or sickness. Not knowing whether I should tell him 'soup's on', I distractedly kept my eyes on him and consequently half the cheese and salad fell off. He'd been listening to Alba playing the piano through closed doors. Helping me pick up the salad said it wasn't bad for

36 *Samuel Beckett, 2 June 1975.*
Silver-point on barium primed board, 65 x 50 cm.

the amount of time she'd been studying. We talked of our trip to England. We mentioned visiting our friend in Ashton. He said Johnson used to live – or was it go – there. Sam knew Oundle. Used to play cricket in Northamptonshire, once against the local team. Talked of Landor's *Imaginary Conversations*. We both recite the quatrain 'I strove with none, for none was worth my strife'; I'd just learned it, but he had a much longer time ago, yet didn't falter. He found the name Walter Savage Landor such a good name. I told him about this friend at Ashton, the entomologist Miriam Rothschild-Lane and her butterflies, and her conclusion that those who succeed too well don't survive, they eat up all the green; she'd said, 'Blessed are the meek.' Sam's reply to this, though not totally agreeing, was 'Moderation'. S. talked about the German translation of *Godot*, and the production, had made the translation more concise, had made the number of steps taken from the tree to the stone parallel the length of the sentence. 'If the first part is longer, and if the total amount of steps to be taken are 18, then for the other 12, let's say, they'd be shorter, 6 steps.' The young boy goes out calmly, doesn't run away. S. had all the actors understand every gesture. 'Nothing gratuitous.' He went on to analyse Lucky's speech, divided into three parts:

The sky, indifferent and cold to human suffering;
Man becoming smaller, all hope taken away;
Earth, throwing up stones, becoming petrified.

I asked if he'd written this down, he said yes. I showed him a paragraph on Rabbi Yehoshua ben Levi, about waiting for the Messiah. To compress it, I added, 'He can't come. That's part of it.' Sam said, 'The essence of it. The waiting.' We talked again about the tragedy of Alberto Giacometti's tree disappearing in the riots of 1968. [It was A. who had given Sam the idea of asking Giacometti to make the tree (Alberto's brother Diego made the leaf), and went with him to Alberto's studio to look at it when it was done.]   37

S. ate very well, finished everything, but wouldn't have dessert. When A. told him it was a children's dessert, a purée of pears, he took some. Happy with the way the children laughed and danced around him, Noga in dark blue pyjamas, the bottom of which kept slipping off; he laughed rather than just grinned, then looked into the fireplace, as I knew he would, having even got the fire going thinking he'd enjoy it as we both recited Landor's quatrain again:

I strove with none, for none was worth my strife:
Nature I loved, and next to Nature, Art:
I warm'd both hands before the fire of life;
It sinks; and I am ready to depart.*

* Written on Landor's seventy-fourth birthday, 30 January 1849, after Dickens and Browning had left him, having come to celebrate. He lived on till 1864.

Mrs Thrale, Mrs Thrale, did you do things like that?

[Added in the margin of this entry that I'd met him the Monday before in the street, outside the Café Marigny on the corner of Boulevard Port Royal and the rue St Jacques. Asked him how he was, noticing the fatigue in his face. I added, 'You look tired.' Said he: 'I'm *very* tired. And how are you?' I was on my way to get the typewriter back and then pick up Alba. Cold raw day. Worries at home. I said, making a face, 'Many things', lifting my head in mock emphasis, 'but one thing we're *not* is tired.' Smile in his eyes. Asks slowly, in same rhythm, mock replique, mock question, 'And *why* aren't you tired?' I said we were too fed up. Both of us laughed. Reminded him we'd be seeing each other Friday night. We said good-bye, he kissed me warmly, I floated away.]

13 January 1976 He talked about Sidney Smith, he had been re-reading him. Tennyson, Johnson and Goldsmith. Was happy we liked *Tryst*. Wondered what we thought of the idea of a woman playing it, Billie in particular.

30 December 1977 Recited a distich:

Sitôt sorti de l'hermitage No sooner out of the hermitage
ce fût le calme après l'orage came the calm after the storm

94

37 *Left to right*: Avigdor, Sam and Alberto Giacometti. In the sculptor's studio, 1961, viewing the tree made by Alberto and Diego Giacometti for *Waiting for Godot*. Photo © Georges Pierre.

Talked about Jocelyn, Billie Whitelaw. Leonardo. A. talked about changing '*paliers*', mind-sets; people find it easy to do in music (listen differently to music than to speech) impossible to do in writing and painting (to switch from using the eye in the street to using it in front of a painting), but he'll stick to nature in order to escape the fiction.* Sam: 'All writing is a sin against speech-lessness. Trying to find a form for that silence. Only a few, Yeats, Goethe, those who lived for a long time, could go on to do it, but they had recourse to known forms and fictions. So one finds one-self going back to *vieilles compétences** – how to escape that. One can never get over the fact, never rid oneself of the old dream of giving a form to speechlessness.' '*Vieilles compétences*' ('the old adroitness').

* Painting from observation as opposed to painting from recollection.

* 'Know-how', as opposed to the creative act.

About his new work, said '[the problem is] *qui est qui*. One would have to invent a new, a fourth person, then a fifth, a sixth – to talk about *je*, *tu*, *il*, never. *Qui est qui*. The logical thing to do would be to look out the window at the void. Mallarmé was near to it in the *livre blanc*. But one can't get over one's dream.' A. said, 'Because of energy.' Sam: 'And entropy. And between these two we know which one wins.' A.: 'That's being.' I: 'Being isn't logical.' Sam repeated: 'A sin against speechlessness. When one tries to say it, one uses the old forms, one tells all kinds of stories.'

Told him about our daughters inventing a comrade they called Agnès, always getting into trouble and called upon to wash the dishes or clean up their rooms! He remembered when, being very young, playing in the garden, he invented companions to play with.* We told him about some of Agnès's escapades. He understood. Said, '*C'est elle la révolutionnaire.*'

See Endgame.

15 March 1978 Sam a bit melancholy. Becomes animated when talking about John Calder's Labrador bitch, how he deposited her, together with his coat, at the Hyde Park Hotel while they had lunch. [Sam had written to us about Calder's dog from London in 1964, saying she walked him from Hyde Park to Mayfair.]

38

A. shows him two Eichendorff poems, one of which he reads aloud. A. asks him to take the volume, there's a bleak 'No, I tore up I don't know how many about a hundred cards and photographs, they have no meaning to anyone.' Later, Schubert, 'let's have a *Lied* or two'. Gretchen's song. 'The most marvellous.' Schumann next,

'*Ich hat' im Traum geweinet*' ('I had wept in my sleep') A. 'Do you want it before or after?' Retorts, 'Neither', with a grin. Then the *Schwanengesang*. After that, Brahms's '*Immer leiser wird mein Schlummer*' ('Ever fainter is my sleep'). Can sing to most of the Brahms, Schumann, Schubert *Lieder*. 'Couldn't work much in Tangier. Took long walks on the beach, strong wind, even rain.'

7 July 1978 Came with presents. Heine's autobiography. Joyce catalogues from Buffalo. Record of German poets. He had told us about Joyce's remark on Dante's use of the verb *essere—fui, fu, fummo*—how, in those lines, it sounded regret for the past. Was it from Paolo and Francesca? The section 'In its leaves we read no more'? (As always, from Cary's translation.) He quoted Canto V, line 142; he specified the source, thinking it the one I meant, in English, knowing I didn't know Italian:

'E caddi, come corpo morto cade.'

Then, corroborated what I'd read in Ariosto's *Orlando Furioso*:

*'E cada, come corpo morto cade.'**

* 'And like a corpse, fell as a dead body falls'; '(And when I saw him,) I fell at his feet as a dead body falls.' Canto II, 55.

On to Heine, whose last act before committing himself 'to a long confinement due to invalidity', was to go see the *Venus de Milo* at the Louvre. Talk about Heine and Venus. About Goethe's writings on art Sam was not as appreciative, although, A. remarked, his work on colours was very good for the time. Sam talked of painting and poetry, Proust's Bergotte, before his death, going to see the Vermeer 'View of Delft', his *'un petit pan de mur jaune...si bien peint...comme une précieuse oeuvre d'art chinois'* ('a small patch of yellow wall...so well painted...like a precious work of Chinese art'). Referred to a record of German poets, but no Trakl on record, liked Trakl very much. Dinner. (A salad of purslane, 'good English word'.) Hans Hotter singing *Schwanengesang*. The way he sang *Doppelgänger*. We put it on three times, sang it together. Third time Hotter's rendition of the wringing of hands 'sounded a bit forced'. He called Jocelyn, ending off the conversation with 'Please God we meet soon, and that you have good news.' Jocelyn had mentioned that Peggy Ashcroft would be hurt if Billie were to play it now (*Happy Days*). May have to put it off for two years. Sam: 'Can't hurt Peggy over something like that. What does it matter, two years.'

19 April 1979 First he talked about the problem with the plumber. Then his excitement over working with Billie. Sees her dressed

London 1.7.

Chers amis

Bien arrivé. Faiblesse du
côté des poubelles. Tout à
refaire et très peu de temps.
Travail sur le plateau à partir
de dimanche. Pat et Jack —
beaucoup de perdu mais pas
d'inquiétude. Complications

à N.Y. Possible que ça soit
de nouveau remis. J'espère
que non. En finir. Très
beau temps. Vu personne.
Aucune envie. Sors le soir
avec la chienne Calder. Elle
me promène — Hyde Park
et Mayfair. Du bon tennis
à la TV. Me rêve tout ça,
ininterrétable.
                Affectueusement

98

38
*London, 1.7.64**
Chers amis

   Bien arrivé. Faiblesse du côté des poubelles. Tout
à refaire et très peu de temps. Travail sur le plateau à
partir de dimanche. Pat et Jack - beaucoup de perdu.
Mais pas d'inquiètude. Complications à N.Y. Possible
que ça soit de nouveau remis. J'espère que non. En finir.
Très beau temps. Vu personne. Aucune envie. Sors le
soir avec la chienne Calder. Elle me promène – Hyde
Park et Mayfair. Du bon tennis à la TV. Un rêve tous ça,
ininterprétable.
   Affectueusement
   Sam

* Date on postal stamp.

London, 1.7.64
Dear friends

   Arrived safely. Dustbins inadequate. Everything
has to be done over again and very little time. Work on
stage starting Sunday. Pat and Jack – fallen off a lot. But
not to worry. Complications in N. Y. Possibility of being
delayed yet again. Hope not. Get it over with. Very fine
weather. Have seen no one. Not the slightest desire. Go
out in the evening with Calder's dog. She walks me – Hyde
Park and Mayfair. Good tennis on TV. All this a dream,
uninterpretable.
   Love
   Sam

in black; Willie in black hat with pink ribbon. Her parasol pink. Talked of his walking through the park in London. Tragic decline of Pat Magee. Pat's drinking problem. We reminded him that even in 1964 he and Jackie MacGowran had drunk so much after celebrating *Endgame* that they ended up asleep on the floor in our flat. Winnie misquotes 16 times. Recites 'Go forget me, why should sorrow fling its shadow o'er...' as well as Milton. Then Goldsmith's epitaph:

> From misery furled
> a bookseller's hack
> not for the world
> would he come back.

Spoke of Goldsmith's misery and bad luck. Then more about Winnie's misquotes. Then 'I call to the eye of the mind'. Beautiful recitation, wind rhyming with kind, as in 'Blow, blow, thou winter wind'. More of Yeats. Mentioned the presumption of B. sending him birthday greetings. Again asked about Alba's back [she had scoliosis]. Didn't think he could take time off to go to Jocelyn's farm, 'want to work, looking forward to it, so long in preparation for it, living with it'. He spoke as impatiently as a farmer trying to gather his harvest before the bad weather sets in – a few 'I shouldn't think so's'. Talked about the Louvre. Had been there with A. in March to see his show on Poussin's *The Rape of the Sabines*.*

31 July 1979 Noga answered the door, he scooped her up, they smiled at each other. Talked about Billie's success, people queuing up as far as the underground, now she had to go to Germany to play a short role in her husband's [Robert Müller's] autobiographical film, would do a Greek cycle back in London. S. looked at reviews of A.'s show in *Time* and *Newsweek*; read them quickly, avidly, his eye skipping some lines to get the gist, said Robert Hughes's article was the best. Noga came in while he was looking up Rudolf Schmitt in *Oxford Pocket Dictionary of Music*,

* Nearly fifteen years earlier Sam had made notes on the end pages of a selection of Poussin's letters which Avigdor had given him, *Lettres et propos sur l'art*, edited by Anthony Blunt for the series *Miroirs de l'art*, Hermann, Paris, 1964. In an extremely careful hand, exceptionally clear, Sam listed phrases and letters he was especially struck by.

couldn't find it. He sat near her and stroked her hair and cheek. At table, Haut Brion 1964. After a few seconds, he looks at us and says, 'Nectar'. Ate well, down to the cheese. I asked why do we say, about marvellous things of the earth, 'divine'? He replied in a low voice, so I wasn't sure if he said 'never say it' or 'it's not personal', probably 'never say it' – couldn't hear it clearly.

A. asked about the new text. Twenty pages in English. Was it a text he had reworked and reworked. 'No, I put my foot on it.' Noga came in with chessboard, he and A. sometimes played, but he'd promised this time to teach her. A. wanted to put on Schumann, Janet Baker singing *Liederkreis* while Sam started the first elementary lesson of chess. Sam and Noga: their two heads together, a 74-year-old and a 10-year-old; lots of hair on the two of them, silver and dark, he thin, bent over, explaining, she gold and curly, bent over, listening to his explanations. Voices came over to me in the kitchen, his like someone pointing out something on the radio, high pitched, slow, very careful, articulating each step with tremendous seriousness and patience. His attitude – 'watch out for the pawns, they can outdo the king'. Played a few opening moves, warned her again of the dangers of each step, told her the name of one particular check move. She goes off to bed, kissing him good-night. A., drawing very rapidly, managed to draw the two of them playing chess. (This time Sam was unaware, but even when he is aware that A. is drawing him, he never has to be told not to move. He continues to sit or stand in the same attitude, as unselfconsciously as possible. Whenever he was told he looked so much like the portraits Arikha had drawn of him, he'd smile and say, 'I try my best.')

Immediately on to Schumann, didn't have quite the effect he expected. Going back to chess, I asked about the king, he said 'only at the end can he use his power, the queen is all-powerful'. He passionate about it: 'It's marvellous. Inexhaustible.' I asked if there were parallels in life. He said, 'No, no parallels in life. One has to see six steps ahead.' [After this initiation, Sam brought Noga books on chess on several occasions.] Talked about Brahms, he not very enthusiastic, except for – exceptions (grin), the *'Immer leiser wird mein Schlummer'*. 'It's marvellous, one of the most marvellous songs.' A. put on Hans Hotter singing *Der Leiermann**, S. preferred Fischer-Dieskau, 'at the end there's a real cry, he cries out'. We put on Fischer-Dieskau to compare. At the end, the cry, a shudder. S. looked at me, there it was. Nodded. Too moved to talk.

About Brahms again, how he sometimes goes on and on. [We listened often, for many years before that, to Brahms's trios and his sextets, which he loved.] Gerald Moore's art. A.: 'Why do people talk against someone just because he's great?' I: 'Schubert, great from the first note.' S.: 'but sometimes he goes on too long, at the end.' Talk about Con and Marion. S.: 'She has great vitality.' I: 'and Con enjoys so many things.' S.: 'He enjoys looking on from the sidelines. Watchlines.' A.: 'A voyeur?' S.: *'un voyeur voyant* ['a clairvoyant/ onlooking *voyeur'*]. He told me long ago that he preferred looking on.' A.: 'I don't know what I am. I observe, but I don't know. I can only observe.' S.: 'don't know where I am – not watching.' I: 'the pitcher, the ball?' S.: 'I don't know where I am but I'm not only observing.' A.: 'He's very lucky, Con, not embittered.' S.: 'Yes, he never tried. Knew enough to know he couldn't.'

21 June [*1980?*] Talked about *Purgatory* Canto XVII, p. 179. He mentioned reading the correspondence of Gottfried Benn. Talked about my poems. (For integrity's sake, will mention what he said about them – found them moving, strange, and so on – because I can counterbalance those words with the contrary: he asked to meet me at a café on Boulevard Montparnasse, I think it was La Coupole, to talk about two of my poems he'd wanted to see the week before. He looked so unhappy, his eyes lowered so long, that I had to take his hand across the table and say, 'You can tell me it's no good, Sam; I didn't think you'd like it in the first place.' He looked up, then, immensely relieved, said, 'You see, it's too long, the woman, the daughter, there's too much in there.' I left him a calmer and happier man that day, and I broke out with herpes on the cheek the next. Therefore, when he said,

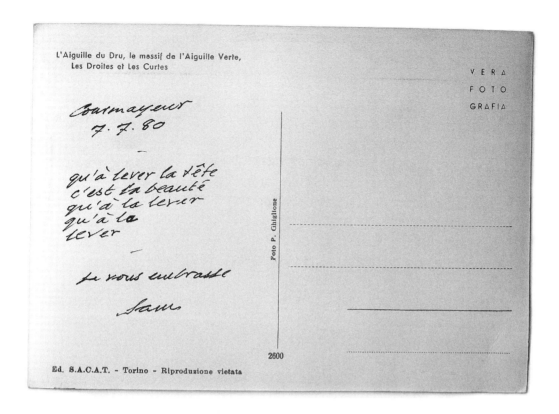

Courmayeur
7. 7. 80

—

qu'à lever la tête
c'est la beauté
qu'à la lever
qu'à la
lever

—

je vous embrasse

Sam

on some other occasions, how he was moved by my poems, I had
to accept it as his true opinion, as unimaginable as that was to
me. Nothing, no old friend, no one dear or particularly vulner-
able, could ever make him say something he didn't believe.)

S. said about a certain publisher that he doesn't keep his authors'
heads above water. I: *'Après moi le déluge?'* S.: *'Pendant moi le
déluge.'* ('After me, the flood?' 'During me, the flood,' meaning
'I'm all right, Jack,' or, 'Don't care what happens to others'); spoke
worriedly about A.'s need for information/ research. Said he himself had also been too long away from his work, would now bring
it with him to Italy, had finally got a paragraph down. Spoke about
Marion [Con had died the previous October], 'She's all right now
when she's with other people, not so much when she's alone.'

7 July 1980 Got a card from him from Courmayeur: *'qu'à lever la
tête/ c'est la beauté/...qu'à la/ lever... Je vous embrasse,* Sam*

39 A card from Courmayeur.

39

* 'Just to raise the head/ that is the
beauty/ just to raise/ it Love Sam'

40 *Sam Beckett playing chess with Noga, 28 October 1980.*
Hard graphite on wove paper, 24 x 32.7 cm.

28 October 1980 Came to dinner. Another chess game with Noga; A. draws the two of them playing. Took no other notes this evening.

19 April 1981 Alba left with her school group this morning. We tell him about his text *Mal vu mal dit*, our enthusiasm for it. He was happy. I mention having read of writers – and it must be true of composers – writing in rhythm according with their pulse and respiration. S.: 'In that case I would be panting. *Halétant.*' (I found the text later, after he'd left, of the physician and 'maker of verses' Oliver Wendell Holmes, 'who suggested that verse stress is related to pulse beat, and claimed that the rate of a poet's respiration influenced the length of his lines, which may account for the difference between the rhythm of Homer and Herrick'.)* Sam quoted

* The American poet Peter Viereck has also written about the biological basis for metre, stress, rhyme, etc. in poetry, in several publications.

Dante, *Purgatory* Canto XIII, 89: '*Sì che chiaro/ Per essa scenda dalla mente il fiume*' ('That the stream of memory may flow down clearly through it'). Joyce heard fluidity in *fiume* (not only regret for the past, as S. had told us earlier). At table we tell him of Paul Scofield in Brook's film of *King Lear*. Sam said he used 'vile jelly' in his new text, *Ill Seen Ill Said* – 'Ill and Mal both in English and French are adjective and noun.' He'd been rereading *King Lear*. 'Impossible to stage.' About Chekhov – 'How bad the translations are, yet somehow, *ça passe*, the mood, the atmosphere.' He expressed great admiration. I asked whether the quality transmitted was regret, nostalgia, like in Chopin? Didn't answer, wasn't willing to talk about Chopin just then. We were going to listen to *Winterreise* and *Schwanengesang*. He was all ready, taut, holding one side of the record, rubbing his mouth. Loved Hotter's interpretation. When we came to the *Doppelgänger* (to the poem by Heine), eyes lifted, then down, then tears, fierce nod of head. No words. Back to the *Leiermann*. Said: 'The principle is all wrong. But a miracle happened.' When I asked how the same words would have been without the music, or vice-versa, S. exclaimed: 'But Heine is a great poet,' said with absolute conviction.

After dinner we accompanied him home [he didn't live very far from us, which is one reason people who wanted to get in touch with him sometimes dropped their letters into our mailbox]. We mention the difficulty of having girls, of being a girl, the anxieties that having adolescent daughters entails, he asked, 'Is she affectionate?', a surprising question. Told him I found Jeremiah's imagery objectionable about women being wanton, abandoned, menstrual, but maybe he had an adolescent daughter. He laughed, 'Jeremiads'. (Have learned since that Jeremiah had no children.) We walked on, reciting 'Since brass nor stone nor earth nor boundless sea', all very moved, Sam discounted the last two lines, saying, 'They're unnecessary, like some of Schubert's endings.' But added, 'I wouldn't have minded writing that.' I repeated, 'Oh, how can summer's honey breath hold out,' he said, 'No one ever wrote like him.' I: 'Hard to believe he was a human being.' A. said, perhaps he

* A. tells of *L'Idée du peintre parfait* by Roger de Piles (1699) which was published in the 1725 Trévoux publication of Félibien, falsely attributed to Félibien...

† Professor of English Literature and Civilization at the Sorbonne, an early admirer of Beckett.

did not write all that is attributed to him.* S. came back to *Lear*: 'Impossible to stage.' We'd talked about Jean-Jacques Mayoux[†] earlier at dinner, Sam said he'd run into Suzanne Mayoux, ohc'd been laid up with bad hip arthritis. For the first time in many years he remarked on what I was wearing, a loose, green and white Laura Ashley print dress. He said, 'That's a very nice dress you're wearing.' Told him it was English material, made in Wales. He said, 'Nice and sacky.'

29 April 1981 At the Café Français. He was dissatisfied with work in Stuttgart. Television not a medium he can handle, too many machines; ventilator audible; 'someone proposed having five people use fans – a *plaisanterie*' ('joke'); and continued about the lights: 'once the white red green blue are on the costumes, all at once, doesn't give the right effect; music not right'. Decided to hand it over to his assistant, not direct it himself. A. spoke about Ingres. S. asked again about Alba. All the mail and cables of birthday wishes fell on him like a torrent. Will run away to Tangier in September because of Festival. Spoke to Billie in Buffalo [doing *Rockaby*], went very well. Asked about Jocelyn. Told him about the concert tonight. A. and S. spoke about *Beethoven im Gespräch*; repeated some of their favourite passages, as when Goethe and Beethoven were strolling and suddenly saw the empress, the dukes and the entire court coming in their direction; Beethoven said, 'Let's not make way for them,' whereas Goethe did, and bowed; Beethoven walked straight ahead and the court, splitting into two, made way for him; and how he'd receive questions on paper and answer *à tue-tête* – at the top of his voice; S. said it was an interesting idea for a play; we encouraged him to pursue this idea. Beethoven a bit too heroic for him, as was Joyce, and indeed, 'their lives, in which they continued their work in spite of formidable obstacles, were heroic'. S. quoted Joyce's 'and I will forge in the smithy of my soul...' then both A. and S. continued about Beethoven, Napoléon. I: 'If I dared, I'd see myself more like Schubert.' S.: 'I – rock-bottom.' A.: '*Sans artifice*' ('unpretentious'). S.: '*dénudé*' ('bare'). A.: 'Like Socrates bare-foot in the snow.' S.:

'I didn't know that.' Then Sam again cautioned A. on the danger of research to an artist. Before that, on Beethoven, A.: 'How sad that Beethoven didn't know how much Ingres and others admired him.' S. told of what Beethoven said when Schubert's *Lieder* were brought to him eight days before his death – *'Wahrlich, in dem Schubert wohnt ein göttlicher Funken!'* ('Truly, there's a divine spark in Schubert'). Also: *'Dass dieser noch viel Aufsehen in der Welt machen werde.'* ('One day this man will make a great stir in the world.') The great pity is that Schubert, who revered him, didn't know, was all alone, isolated. S.: 'except for his friends'. I: 'He had no echo, no response. Would echo have been important?' S.: *'Si on se rend compte de l'écho, on est fichu.'* ('If you are aware of the echo, you're done.')

31 May, 1981 At the Café Français. Slightly unshaven, grisly, tired. Overwhelmed with requests by the new Culture minister, Jack Lang, for a few lines for Mitterrand's inauguration, request transmitted via the chief curator of the Musée National d'Art Moderne, Germain Viatte – because of Viatte's services in the lending of paintings for the Paris-Paris show. A. said one of Bram's (van Velde) oils looked tattered, as though it wouldn't hold out, Sam said impishly, 'I like it that way.' S. spoke of problems with the Stuttgart television crew; A. suggested phosphorescent paper for light effects, S. wrote it down, asked of Alba, 'She doesn't hate me?' (had been asked to come along). Then about tickets for Madeleine Renaud's performance [in *Oh les beaux jours*]. Then his new poem:

> Head on hands
> hold me
> unclasp
> hold me.

Then about forthcoming legislative elections, when A. said it would be all right as long as Mitterrand doesn't have to succumb to Communist pressure; S. said, *'Et qu'est-ce que ça fera, quelques communistes? Il y a quand-même des gens dans ce pays qui le sont.* ('What can that matter, a few communists? After all there are people in this country who are communists.') But agreed that Marchais wasn't the right person, '*les intellectuels communistes sont tous contre lui – il n'est pas bien.*' ('The communist intellectuals are all against him – he's no good.')

7 September 1981 S. arrived promptly at 8. As usual, he waited behind the door before ringing, not wanting to arrive a minute too early or too late. As usual, we waited on the other side of the door for him to ring. In the studio, looked at A.'s work, at the portrait from the back (A.'s back). Then at the still life. As I expected, no immediate reaction to the still life with blue pitcher. Then: 'Marvellous. *Extraordinaire,*' and back to the portrait. Alba and Noga came out of their room. Took Alba by her shoulders, spread her hair [straightened] between his fingers, smiling, said, 'Is this Alba?' While A. went upstairs to the loggia to get more paintings, Sam slipped into my hands the text he'd written for A.* together with Eugene Istomin's letter. [There was a secret project, organized by Eugene, for the publisher, Jovanovitch, to bring out a special edition, and originally Sam had planned to write about A.'s work for him, but decided to write a text about seeing, instead, which became *Ceiling*, as having much more to do with A.'s approach. It ended up being published by Pierre Berès.] Talk. Sat down to dinner. I'd looked quickly through *Ceiling.* He said: 'Will it do? Has nothing to do with anything. Hope it's all right.'

At table, talked about the plays in the festival, told Alba about Rick Cluchey acting in his play in prison. Ate everything. [Whenever there was fish, he'd crack the bones and actually swallow them – saying they were a great source of calcium.] Laughed boyishly along with the two girls when they heard that he and A. had gone to see Donald Duck and Woody Woodpecker, once, in the fifties, when S. had been very depressed. He talked about his bent fingers (Dupuytren's disease), and A. gave him a hand spring for grasping like the one his mother used. Cigars. Talked about Carmi's anthology (*The Penguin Book of Hebrew Verse*)

* This is his English version of the French text: 'I have not ceased to admire, throughout his development, his acuity of vision, sureness of execution and incomparable grasp of the past and the problems that beset continuance. It is perhaps in this double awareness, at once transcended and implicit in his work, that he is in a sense heroically alone' Samuel Beckett, 1982.

41

42

~~Ceiling~~
Somehow again

On coming to the first sight is of white. Some time
after coming to the first sight is of dull white. For
some time after coming to the eyes continue to. When in
the end they open they are met by this dull white. Consciousness eyes to of having come to. When in the end they
open they are met by this dull white. Dim consciousness
eyes bidden to of having come partly to. When in the end
bidden they open they are met by this dull white. Dim consciousness eyes unbidden to of having come partly to. When
in the end unbidden they open they are met by this dull
white. Further one cannot.

On.

No knowledge of where gone from. Nor of how. Nor of
whom. None of whence come to. Partly to. Nor of how. Nor
of whom. None of anything. Save dimly of having come to.
Partly to. With dread of being again. Partly again. Somewhere
again. Somehow again. Someone again. Dim dread born first
of consciousness alone. Dim consciousness alone. Confirmed
when in the end the eyes unbidden open. To this dull white.
By this dull white. Further one cannot.

On.

Dim consciousness first alone. Of mind alone. Alone come
to. Partly to. Then worse come of body too. At the sight
of this dull white of body too. Too come to. Partly to.
When in the end the eyes unbidden open. To this dull white.
Further one –

On.

Something of one come to. Somewhere to. Somehow to. First
mind alone. Something of mind alone. Then worse come body
too. Something of body too. When in the end the eyes unbidden
open. To this dull white. Further –

On.

Dull with breath. Endless breath. Endless ending breath.
Dread darling sight.

41 Manuscript of *Ceiling*, 1981. Beckett hesitated between two titles for this
text, *Ceiling*, as was written on the top line and then crossed out, and *Somehow
again*, as written underneath. The title he kept at the end was *Ceiling*.

42 *Samuel Beckett with cigar, 5 July 1970.*
Brush and sumi ink on coated canvas-paper 35,1 x 27 cm.
Paris, Musée National d'Art Moderne, Centre Pompidou.

– for years he'd heard about Carmi from A. and me and had read his work, but only met him by chance one night in the Men's Room of the Closerie des Lilas, while A. and I were waiting for Sam upstairs. [As Carmi remembered the story, he asked Sam, 'Are you Samuel Beckett?' and Sam, caught off guard, said, 'Yes, so what?', at which point Carmi introduced himself.] S. went into the play-room and played the piano there, then listened to Alba play. Later, after long consideration as to what he'd like to hear, we listened to Schubert's 'Trout' quintet, then the 2nd movement (variations) of *Death and the Maiden*. At first he couldn't remember the name of the poet he knew by heart, said to A., 'You know, the one we talk about a lot, who edited a magazine...' After some hesitation A. guessed that he meant Matthias Claudius. S. found Clifford Curzon in the 'Trout' too dominant at the beginning but not afterwards. He was leaving for Tangier next week to escape the Beckett festival (the Festival d'Automne in Paris due to start in October, of 13 works, discussions, films, etc.). I: 'Couldn't you pretend you weren't here?' S.: 'Can't do that, not fair. So many friends are coming in, Schneider, etc.' I: 'Perhaps you could go away, then come back after two weeks.' S.: 'That would be cheating, I can't do that.' S. walked out with A. (who often walked him home). He was less tired tonight.

13 November 1981 Showed him Noga's new telescope. He looked at it critically, then appraisingly. 'Marvellous.' Flat pronouncement, not a trace of condescension. Alba about to go out for the evening, hithering and thithering. We continued at the table, talking as before about his plays, and he about X.'s performance. X. seems to have learned mostly from other people's comments about Billie's *Rockaby*, her rhythm in the rocking-chair, and so on. Then about how realism is abstract. Painting versus literature.

A. pointed out that painting is just the reverse of literature. As painter, he has to see as well as he can what's outside in order to see, to capture, the inside. Memory obstructs immediacy in painting, whereas, for a writer, memory is most important, the writer has to look inside to get to the truth of what's outside;

what's outside cannot be seen, S. interjected: 'not for one nor for the other', but for the painter it's a necessary condition. Sam listened, one felt he acquiesced profoundly and also understood the difference. 'Literature and painting are like oil and water, and I don't know which is which.' Earlier, speaking about adumbration, he had put it differently: 'like fire and water they are separated by a zone of evaporation'.*

* Quoted by M. Omer in his introduction to the exhibition catalogue, *Samuel Beckett by Avigdor Arikha, A tribute to Samuel Beckett on his 70th birthday*, Victoria and Albert Museum, London, February–May 1976, p. 5.

At table, talked of Top and Kiki, problems of translation. Why German is so hard, for *Mal vu mal dit* no word for both substantive and adjective, the problem in German of verbs at the end. Noga said it was like Latin, S. very attentive to what she said. S. very attentive to what everyone said, sometimes to their discomfiture; made me realize again how people aren't used to being listened to so literally – because they themselves don't listen, but discount half of what's said and extract the general tenor. Not Sam. There was no general tenor and every word counted. Music afterwards. The same problem A. sometimes had of finding the right piece; both he and Sam wanted the Mozart *Fantaisie*. A. looked and looked, couldn't find it, found something else instead, the *Rondo*. Not as good after the first few variations. Then S. talked about Marion's trips, 'running away from her sorrow'. About writers and painting again: A., how few writers really looked at painting, all those writers who talk about painting and don't even go to the Louvre. For a second I felt Sam thought it was directed at him though he didn't say so, but I, and then A. went on to talk about S.'s visual sense, his annotated catalogues from all the museums he'd been to (and had given A.), which may account for his visual originality in the theatre, his choreography. Then S. said he would be going to Ussy.

[As for the Louvre, he did go there, in 1979, in spite of his fear of being recognized, to see A.'s presentation of Poussin's *Rape of the Sabines*; A. took him on a Tuesday, when it was closed to the public. He stayed for a long time. Sam avoided going to public places. Even had to go see the Madeleine Renaud/ Jean-Louis Barrault *Oh les beaux jours* (*Happy Days*) surreptitiously, too often accosted by passers-by. His craggy features, his cheekbones' slopes, had been photographed and admired by Parisians too long for him to escape notice. Which is why he went to restaurants where the waiters, though they knew who he was, were discreet, as at Les Iles Marquises, frequented by boxers and boxing fans, and why he would have people meet him at the Café Français (even there, as we were leaving after a pleasant morning coffee, an American woman whispered in my ear, 'Tell me, is it really Beckett or am I dreaming?'). He stopped going to the Closerie des Lilas once he'd been spotted there – although we three did go late one night, when Sam and A. played chess on a portable set, and Orson Welles came in with a friend. There were only the five of us in that enormous space, nearly midnight, and Welles called out in a stage whisper to his friend, 'That's Beckett over there'; but no one made any move to introduce them, though I had a feeling Sam wouldn't have minded. But he'd been recognizable in Montparnasse for years. Some time in the 1950s, before he became well known, Sam and A. went to have a beer and something to eat at four o'clock in the morning at a *café-tabac* called La Marine. It was open all night, a place where people who had to open their shops early, like butchers and so on, used to go. One of the customers asked Sam casually, 'Are you Samuel Beckett?' Sam was a bit troubled, and before responding he hesitated, then asked where *he* was from. The young man answered, 'Alaska.' When Sam smiled and asked him if he was going back, he said, 'Yes, tomorrow.' Sam politely asked him a few more questions, but the man was discreet and left the two of them alone.]

Tuesday, 22 December 1981 at the Café Français. He was disappointed that Noga wasn't with us. She was still asleep, had stayed up late to watch Louis Jouvet in *Hôtel du Nord*; he had a present for her, *The History of Chess*. Talked about Alba, Edward, his address, Poland – 'terrible' situation there, seemed to agree with A.'s analysis of Solidarity and its demands. Then on to the death of Bram (van Velde). Looked very sad after we talked about it. I think it was the quickness with which we seemed to get used to the idea. Does he imagine for one moment that he is like that? To us? Then about Geer (Bram's brother, also a painter), and his approaching exhibition. Sam had been writing, then stopped, very hard, but took it up again. Talked about Jocelyn (Herbert) and her work for the *Oresteia*, she was coming over in March. Asked about the subject of A.'s lecture at the Ecole des Beaux-Arts, the deficient teaching there. He had ceased to be animated, lively, interested; the quick ready smile when expecting wit to strike vanished once Bram's death came up. Noga should have come. He talked about François Jacob's appearance on television, about life in the womb (which S. had talked about many years earlier, claiming to remember his own birth), how Jacob talked about it as still the greatest mystery, miracle. Then about Arthur Rubinstein in Israel, having a whole forest named after him.

4 November 1982 Came with his briefcase. A present for Noga (Alba, asked about, missed, studying in the United States), the 1785 edition of Johnson's poems; Noga leaped with joy. Drinks. Showed him the record of Elizabeth Schumann, *Nacht und Träume*, which I'd volunteered to try to find for him, and after a long search, finally found, and the score for him to play, thanks to a pianist-friend, Ayala Cousteau. Then he called Jocelyn. Talked about the Seavers visiting him. We told him about seeing Pinter's triple bill in London, and about Judi Dench in *Something Like Alaska* – he'd heard about her. Then on to Dante. Cary's edition. The composition of the circles, Boccaccio's lectures on him, Ugolino, Paolo and Francesca; when Dante heard the story he fainted away. Again quoted Joyce's remark on all of them speaking in the past, beautiful vowels, '*fui, fu, fummo*', then A.'s remark that Manfredi spoke in the present. Sam talks about Belacqua, a smile on his face, described him to Noga; then told her how in Dante all takes place in thirty-six hours. I, about that influencing Joyce to have all the action in *Ulysses* take place over twenty-four hours. Again, he recites *come...cadi*, when Dante heard the story.

Ate everything.* Tonight he liked the fresh salmon, the pineapple. Started a game of chess with Noga. We left them, two heads bowed together, held in their hands, S. pointing out the consequences of her moves patiently. We were going to London for Billie's performance on 9 December, we asked Noga if she wanted to come along, she said she didn't want to miss school. The chess game lasted about 40 minutes, time enough for me to do the dishes, I brought in coffee, he too absorbed to notice. Listened to the Schumann, then to Gundula Janowitz in *Rast, du Krieger*, he very moved by it, whereas several months before had not been so moved. Talk of Johnson, said he kept Johnson's Latin translations as *un livre de chevet*, a bedside book, after I showed him my edition (ordinary) of Johnson's complete poems. He quoted from *The Vanity of Human Wishes*, 'the patron to assail, assailed by patron'; talked about Lord Chesterfield. Then health – A. talked about his lipoma, S. showed him the scar of one that had been removed from his neck, one on his hand. When S. remarked on Noga's understanding of one of his Latin quotes, I asked if he'd also studied Greek, said, 'Alas, no,' he 'had to learn useless things like Physics when my bent was for languages'. He was in good form, warm, not tired, but seemed a bit older, didn't seem to remember things he'd already said, his reactions a bit slower, asked several times about the subject already mentioned. A. (for some reason) couldn't walk back with him. S. would stay only a week in London, had to go to Devon to see his cousin, then visit Patrick's widow. Pat (Magee) was no good at the end – drink had spoiled his memory. Pat's beautiful voice. Told us again, as he had at one of our previous meetings at the Café Français, about how he'd written a piece for Magee just by hearing him on the wireless. Looked at Botticelli drawings, he found them good. I asked about Blake's drawings, he didn't like them, can't get him, doesn't feel them too much. I: 'Really a poet, not a painter.' S.: 'Do you go for his poetry – I don't.' I talked about the chimney sweep, the little black boy, 'O rose thou art sick'. He: 'I don't like it much.' Silent. When we talked about Dante, he recited some lines, then he and I the English 'Abandon all hope...'

*This fact is noted because in his last years he ate even less than the little he usually did. It was sometimes very hard for him to take more than a few bites of anything. His friends noticed what he ate with pleasure, for this reason. He would order certain dishes at certain restaurants: *rognons de veau* – veal kidneys – at Les Iles Marquises; *jambon braisé aux épinards* – braised ham with spinach – at Chez Françoise. Otherwise he'd order fish. As was described earlier, he would crack fish bones between his teeth, and when I served it at home, would invariably assure the girls, who watched him with fascination, that it was very good for them.

43 *Samuel Beckett talking, 26 June 1983.*
Silver-point on coated paper, 15 x 11 cm.

[A few months before the next entry, A. was commissioned by the Scottish National Portrait Gallery to paint the Queen Mother, Sam delighted, but A.'s initial reaction was, 'Why me?' He wasn't British, why not Hockney, why not Freud, he couldn't paint on command, and so forth. But it was *only* because Sam urged him to accept – 'It's in the grand tradition,' he said – that A., with many self-doubts, agreed. And when Sam said that, he meant all the painters who had painted royal figures throughout history, but I couldn't help thinking that he also had in mind Johnson's meeting in 1767 with King George III in the library at Buckingham Palace. About a year later, Sam sent us a newspaper clipping mentioning that there was some talk of A. being asked to paint Prince Philip, but instead A. painted Lord Home.]

24 August 1983 Came in wobbly on his legs – obviously, not from drinking, but simply from ageing. Looked around the stripped walls (we were leaving for New York, to spend a year there, join Alba) taking in the signs of our departure. Put down khaki-green shoulder bag, knapsack style. No socks on, as was his wont in summer (ever since I'd met him). Light beige summer shirt. We showed him Helith's (Israeli translator and poetry editor) translation of *L'Innommable*, showed him his name in Hebrew. We spoke of how the biblical resonances of his English surface in Hebrew, and then about Carmi's translation of *Hamlet*. S. said he'd been reading *King Lear* again, 'Unstageable; wild; scenes and words impossible to stage.' Sorry he hadn't retained Edgar's words before (but he had, as when writing to Jocelyn after George Devine's death, and other times as well): 'They're very important. "The worst is not; so long as we can say, 'This is the worst'."'

Looked so bird-like. We drank Rieussec; interested in A.'s explanation of how the difference of only three weeks makes one Sauternes dry and another sweet. Asked about the Israeli army enlistment for girls, whether Alba would have to go – but she was a citizen only because of A.'s status, not in her own right. We spoke of our trip to Edinburgh: accents, Scottish and Irish. Thence on to Synge. (He had given us Synge's *In Wicklow, West Kerry and*

44 A J. M. Synge poem written down
from memory by Beckett.

Connemara, published in 1919, which he'd bought in 1926.) S.: 'No one spoke like that,' in reference to Synge's attempt to capture folk speech. Talked of *Playboy of the Western World*. Tried to recapture one of Synge's poems. Beautiful motion; head in hands. Got the first line, then the second. Couldn't remember the next few, but did the last two. We brought him a piece of paper, and he got the whole:

44   A silent sinner, nights and days

No human heart to his drew nigh

Alone he wound his wonted ways.

Alone and little loved did die –

And Autumn death for him did choose

A season dank with mist and rain

And took him, as the evening dews

Were settling o'er the fields again.

Spoke of Synge's unhappy love affair with Molly Allgood.* He even left his mother's house, moved to Dublin, to be nearer to her. Why didn't she want him? 'She was reluctant.' Died at thirty-two. Joyce saw him. Synge had a brain tumour, which spread. Joyce died of (badly diagnosed) ulcers, haemorrhage. I read his 1907 preface to *Playboy*. S. smiled at the image 'as fully flavoured as a nut or apple'. He tried to remember what Yeats said about Synge. I finally found it in 'The Municipal Gallery Revisited': 'Synge, that rooted man'. He talked of the correspondence between Synge, Lady Augusta Gregory, Yeats. He admired Synge's plays, and (it suddenly occurred to me) Brouwer's paintings; both Synge and Brouwer, a painter Sam always loved and talked about with A. (as often as about Potter and the cows), his face lighting up when the name was mentioned, drew their characters from the same social class, with the same irony and affection.* Walked him back. When we reached the prison (on the rue de la Santé, near his house), he talked of how he heard them *'hurlant'*, 'shouting', every night during the summer, about the heat, four to a cell. From there to Apollinaire's poems written in the Santé prison. We both recited *'Que les heures passent lentement'* ('How slowly the hours pass'). He remarked on the beautiful play of vowels and consonants. S. was so frail, his bones sticking out through his flesh, that we could have carried him easily if we had to. He spoke of Edward and Felicity (his wife) and Edward's son Christopher. Spoke of Edward's early years at the Conservatoire, we mentioned the twinkle in his eyes. Sam had always been proud of him. About Shakespeare's *Lear*: 'Sometimes there are –' A. interrupted: 'pearls.' S. made a motion with his head, upwards. He'd never seen *Lear* played. Before we left him, he asked about my mother, brothers, A.'s mother. 'Locomotion problems,' I said. He grinned. Was glad he'd found out about the bread at Le Fournil de Pierre.* Liked the translation of the word *lotte*, monk fish. Talked of Augustus John, Jack Yeats and Synge on a trip together. Then of the Abbey Theatre. Had been sent a book about it.

* The younger sister of Sara Allgood, who had been active in the Abbey Theatre and had survived the storm provoked by the first night of Synge's *The Playboy of the Western World.*

* Knowlson writes that Beckett admitted to him to feeling a great debt to Synge, the characters in *Godot* and Synge having something in common, *op.cit*. p. 379.

* The bakery near his house on rue Daguerre.

(Sam ill in the early part of the year. We were still in New York. Came back in July.)

23 December, 1984 Café Français. S. looked more energetic than we expected. Talked about the scandalous ART (American Repertory Theatre) production of *Endgame* at Harvard. We told him about the article in the *Herald Tribune.* His hair cropped, I said he'd had a haircut, 'Yes, I've come to that now,' smiling, 'what will people do next?' Banter. Told him Noga (sleeping late) would join us in a little while. *'Encore faut-il qu'elle sorte du lit.'* ('She'll still have to get' – or, 'That depends whether she gets' – 'out of bed.') He remembered his own difficulties when younger in getting out of bed. Talked about Pierre Berès's book on A. – a tribute, *un témoignage.* About Edward's new house. John working at the BBC. Mentioned Dux's performance, finding the adaptation of Frederick Neumann far superior. Said he'd just met him yesterday. Mentioned Dustin Hoffman only in passing, something about a missed rendez-vous. About ART: one of them called him (Sam) a racist. (Sam had objected to the stage set – a caricature of the bareness he'd wanted – and to the transformation of the mother and father into black actors, when everyone else was white.) Too cold to go to Ussy. Suddenly, about work. How interesting it would be to write a play *about* reading a poem. Surprisingly,

'Let me not to the marriage of true minds,'
and then,

'No longer mourn for me when I am dead.'
Mused a bit on the challenge. I mentioned reading Mandelstam's 'Conversations on Dante'. S. about Mandelstam, 'Oh, he's a *fine* poet!' Noga arrived; hot chocolate, croissants. Sam lit up and interrupted A.'s sentence, drew his face closer to look into hers, still half asleep, still half a child, talked a lot to her. His fingers completely bent, said piano playing would help. Talked about Garfein, appreciated his respect for the texts, but didn't want him to have a monopoly on the work in New York. Rosset had, unannounced, come out with a strongly worded letter to the newspapers about

the ART production. Asked again about Alba. Talked with Noga about horses; he had ridden only once, was knocked off. A. told the story about having a toothache and being thrown by a wild mule he'd mounted to get to the next kibbutz. Laughed more and more the longer we sat. *Tristram Shandy* (I mentioned that Mrs Beeton, in the chapter on 'Domestic Servants' in her *Book of Household Management*, had also said, like Sterne, 'although they do order these things better in France'), he talked enthusiastically about Sterne's freedom and invention. Stayed a half-hour later than usual.

25 January 1985 Café Français. He spoke of his days in the Resistance. Then of how Joyce wrote a letter of introduction for him to Valery Larbaud living outside Vichy. A rich man, generous. 'Went in to see him. Sat in a wheelchair, paralysed. Gave a nice sum,' which Sam paid back, after the war.* How S. began the trip out of Paris, after warning the other members of the cell that they'd been betrayed. Alba came along (who'd written a paper about Larbaud); when S. mentioned Larbaud again, she said, 'Oh, *Barnabooth*.' They would meet and talk about him alone. S. delighted.

*To his estate, as Larbaud had died by then.

2 November 1985 Went to see S. Bad cold, red nose when we arrived, less red when we left. Hard to talk to at first, but gradually opened up. When A. said, 'No more research, catalogues or films,' after he'd finished the next two, S. said: '*Il faut retrouver l'ignorance*' ('You've got to get back to ignorance'). About all that other work: '*C'est très dangereux.*' He talked about G. less enthusiastically, disagreed with some work he had done. Hoffman again. About Claude Simon winning the Nobel Prize, he was very glad for Jérôme (Lindon, the publisher).* Through Lindon got Lang (the minister) to help in sending money to Sam's niece for an operation – a kind of scoliosis; the money got there the same day! The first one didn't work well, the second successful; she married afterwards, remained in Washington. Talked about new work: a man hears noises inside; the same ones at the same

*In the fifties and sixties Claude Simon used to live across the street from A., and would come every day at five sharp. For his *La route des Flandres* he took up A.'s suggestion for an epigraph from Leonardo: 'While I thought I was learning to live, I was learning to die.' Started off as a painter.

pitch outside, when they should have been louder. A clock, a cry. He answered tersely about Suzanne – wasn't well, no. Closed his face. We talked about (Pierre) Chabert, Tophoven (his German translator since 1953), Dutilleux, whom he'd met once with Mihalovici. The music in the café is suddenly César Franck. (Before that, the usual tapes of Häendl, Bach, Tchaikovsky.) Expressed displeasure. 'What's that awful music?' I asked what made the piece so bad – too weepy? S.: 'Too academic.' Talked about Mallarmé; couldn't read his prose but said there were some marvellous poems. Apologized for not seeing Istomin. He had indeed met Albee several times (after the Budapest congress). Havel released from jail again.

Two dates: 2 December or end of November 1986: Last evening out. Came to dinner. Out at night after two years. Alba and Noga there. Looked around. Brown beret.* Talked of the students' strike. Talked about Billie – she was supposed to come to the *Alliance Française* but couldn't make it; about Pierre Chabert. Came to language. Talked about idioms. I mention that new words keep coming in, then disappear, give trivial examples: twit, twerp, nerd. S. in a very sad, low voice, 'How hard to keep up. One speaks like one used to. Language gone.' I: 'Not yours, not gone.' S.: 'Language gone. Heart gone.' At this the girls and I shout out together, 'No!' We decide therefore to read from the Psalms, show how language doesn't go just because of age. I brought out the King James, A. the Hebrew Bible. 'You read,' he said to me. I refused. 'You read, Sam.' Almost shyly, he began, slowly, 'The Lord is my shepherd, I shall not want,' tears in his, our eyes. A. reads the Hebrew. Unutterably moving.

Leave the table; listen to Edward's tape of Telemann. Then the *Doppelgänger,* then the *Leierman, Nacht und Träume.*

18 April, 1987 [probably at the Café Français but was not noted] Thinner than before. The slightly sun-burned yellow look of sick people. His blue eyes brilliant. Blue like David Somerset's, smiling at the corners. Dark green jacket (he said snot-green, like

* Sam was both elegant and very independent in his tastes. He used to wear old-fashioned spectacles, the kind children wore. The rim was made of a white flexible metal layered with black Bakelite – circa 1956–7 – which he would peel off. He was probably one of the first to wear round rimless glasses.

Joyce), plaid green, brown and blue trousers, dark blue turtleneck sweater. Had dressed especially. First fine day, could venture out. Jocelyn there, too. Smile appearing and disappearing in his eyes. Talked about the anthology. Three poems for Barney (Rosset). Clinic in St Marcel. Awful hospital food. Jocelyn remembered having to bring George (Devine) food to the hospital. He asked about the Royal Court, David Gotthard as director. He'd received a clipping about A.'s show in Los Angeles. Looked long and gladly at each of us.

9 February 1989 4.30 p.m. In the old-people's home, Le Tiers Temps. We walk through the sad-looking house. The television is blasting away to old ladies, mainly, with steel-coloured hair, canes, hardly watching at all. Young secretaries smile us through to his door. He opens it, eyes a bit red from drinking, never saw him before at this hour with red eyes. A half-full glass in his hands, Bushmill's on the table, ashtray. Hesitates before taking cigar. As sometimes, hard to talk to at the beginning, then gets easier, lighter. Talks about Jocelyn, Billie, Garfein. More feelingly, about Johnson, the book by Walter Jackson Bate I'd given him. Asks urgently if he can keep it. Likes the index especially. The Oxford episode, the shoes, Williams, Tetty refusing her favours and drinking gin, S. is himself again. Cradled in silence like a cat and as attentive as one; everything considered, beautifully dressed, beautiful to look at. Then the phone rings, it's Suzanne, he asks, *'Je peux te rappeler? Dans un quart d'heure? Avigdor est là.'* ('Can I call you back? In a quarter of an hour? Avigdor's here.') Crash, bang. She hangs up on him. Comes back, sits at the edge of his chair, like one of his own characters, perhaps Joe in *Eh Joe*. Makes a show of answering questions but eyes swerve to the phone as in a movie with obvious directions to cameraman to follow the movement. Obviously in torment trying to follow the conversation but really wanting to get to phone. (Suzanne was not well that year.) A. goes on but I interrupt, 'Would you like us to leave?' straightforward 'Yes I would.' I say I understand and I do. Kiss, leave him. Understood too well that hang-up crash bang. Sam had said before the call that he could not go back home, would not be able to help Suzanne who was sick, would be in her way, she needed to be taken care of. But the doctor said he could go to Ussy in the spring. Doctor took him there one fine day in his car, all fixed up for him, the farmer's wife would look after him, there was a caretaker for the house. (Written Feb. 18th.)

31 August 1989 Again to Le Tiers Temps. We go with the girls. Outer rooms spruced up a bit, lighter, white walls. New chairs and tables, new sofas, same old women waiting to turn on the television, they salute us – is it recognition or custom? – or to have something to do? (Apparently, custom.) S. in beige-brown pants, green-grey turtleneck. (Everyone always noticed what he wore, he dressed very carefully, elegantly.) Sombre at first, greeted us with a kiss. Gradually relaxed. Had his whiskey, Jameson's. 'Now I take it neat.' Talked of Edward, of his other guests, mentioned Billie. Had seen the Bishops, the young Irishman working with Barry McGovern, then spoke of K. How did it go? 'I was apprehensive but he seems to have calmed down a bit, doesn't hold forth so much.' Talked to Alba and Noga, then to A. about his show. About his living arrangements (which all his friends found excruciating): 'Here it's all laid out. I'd need more help if I were to move.' Would see the neurosurgeon, who'd recommended a series of five tests – five over as many days. About *oligo-élements* (trace elements), mentions Edith Fournier. Then Yeats, and Yeats's father who stayed in New York for seventeen years; Joyce's admiration for Yeats, the showy wreath he sent to his funeral. 'He liked to make that sort of gesture.' Surprisingly, went on to say that Yeats had written some great poems – hitherto had never qualified his praise, would never have said 'some'. Went on to say, 'some especially good – "The Tower",' recited, as he had after Con's cremation,

> The death of friends, or death
> Of every brilliant eye
> That made a catch in the breath –
> Seem but the clouds of the sky

About old people – said Yeats had written a good poem about old age, 'a tattered thing'. Then his own

  Age is when to a man
  huddled over the ingle...

then another one from the addenda to *Watt*. Then Goethe, in relation to A.'s recalling Gryphius, both of them reciting

  *Bedecke Deinen Himmel, Zeus**   * 'Cover your sky, Zeus'

then

  No longer mourn for me when I am dead,

skipping a few words, but still entire. Then Keats's 'pouring forth thy soul in such an ecstasy'. Then about Yeats's behaviour to Sean O' Casey, he'd refused *The Silver Tassie* (for the Abbey Theatre, but S. didn't specify, thought I'd know). S. had recently received a letter from O'Casey's widow and daughter, working in the theatre. At the mention of Morandi S. said, 'Yes, a great painter. Did good things.' A. talked about getting a high from coffee, excellent coffee in Bologna, in connection with Morandi (who lived in Bologna, from which we'd just returned); but A. doesn't know if   * The 'high'.
it* points north or south. What direction does whiskey point to, A. asks. S.: 'It points to Ireland.' Found it harder to walk, needed a cane. Whenever he walked back to the flat, was stopped by people who knew him, who asked him all kinds of questions. Had worked out in his mind other walks. Would take la rue Jean Dolent behind the Santé, used to take avenue René Coty when it was quiet, now it's less quiet. About poets dying young. Keats, Shelley (on this subject he'd mentioned Trakl to A.). Heard there was a good Irish poet, Seamus Heaney; listened with great interest when I said I liked his work very much, and talked about it, and Patrick Kavanagh. When A. suggested he had a play in the old woman talking to herself outside his window, S. said she talked

interminably. We told him about the bulbul found and nursed by someone at the Israel Museum, the bird lived there now, S. mentioned the falcons nesting in the belfry of Notre Dame, hears them on their way to Montrouge, they make a sound like a dog, strange. Garfein, Calder, his problems with keeping his office. S. got tired, stretched, but said it was good to – A. interrupted, thinking he meant we should go – but S. meant, to get a chance to talk about poetry. Asked about mine, I told him about the American critic who had said my problem was that I had nothing much to do with most of American poetry. S. said, 'That's not bad.' I said, 'But he meant it in a very dismissive way.' S.: 'That's not dismissive.'* We left at 6.10.

11 December 1989 A call from Edith Fournier (a friend of Suzanne's who had nursed Suzanne* in her last illness and was now nursing Sam), telling us more about Sam's state. She repeated some of what Edward had said to us. Told us that Sam, in his delirium, said he saw A. walking on the wall, and also '*Je m'inquiète pour Anne*' ('I'm worried about Anne' – meaning my eye trouble*). To think that he thought of us in his delirium. She then said he recited from Verlaine and Tennyson. It happened last Wednesday, found on the bathroom floor. Think it's a cerebral lesion. When A. had spoken to him that same night, his speech had been very unclear, mumbling, as though he'd drunk too much, which he probably had. Yet even in this conversation, he had come out with two lines:

> *Le médecin nage,*
> *le malade coule.**

12 December 1989 E. F. called again. Yesterday he could take only a few spoonfuls of apple sauce. This time recited nursery rhymes, Edith Fournier thought, and a bit of Tennyson. We feel as though we are being kept from him (everyone excluded but Edward), we are indeed not allowed to visit him. Three weeks ago he talked about Alba and Noga; Martha (Fehsenfeld) told us so on the phone.

* The poems that the critic dismissed as un-American appeared in London with the Enitharmon Press a year later.

* And who died that same year on 17th July.

* Herpes of the cornea.

* 'The doctor swims,/ the patient drowns' – a play on words: his doctor's name was Coulamy.

Attentive even in his weakness. The great gift he has of friendship. Each one different, everyone trying to grab a few minutes of his recognition. Even in delirium recites poetry. As when he was in the clinic after his cataract operation. Verlaine, Apollinaire. Yesterday Keats.

16 December 1989 Edward, his sister Caroline, the haematologist-doctor and recent friend, Eoin O'Brien, coming today. How to explain the momentous difference he makes in the world. His head crammed with Dante, Voiture, Keats, Apollinaire. The press already hovering, their obituaries no doubt ready. His recovery must be a setback for them. Edward let us come to see him a few days later. He was asleep? Unconscious? We saw the paperback he'd been reading, on a chair, *Sylvia Beach and the Lost Generation*, by Noel Riley Fitch. Was it the last book he read? Certainly not the last lines he called 'to the eye of the mind'.

22 December 1989 Edward calls. It has happened.

Edward asks us to come to the funeral, 26 December. Marion, Josette Hayden, Barbara Bray with her daughter Chechina,* Edward, his sister, some of Suzanne's friends and family, Jérôme Lindon and his wife; ten in all*...Buried, as he'd wanted, near Suzanne.

We go there several times that first week. On one occasion we find a yellow Métro ticket on the tombstone, on which someone has written in small letters: 'Godot will come.'

22 December 1999 Tenth anniversary of his death, Kiki (Erika Tophoven) goes to the cemetery, no one else there (a street bearing Sam's name is being inaugurated not far away, and we're on the train to London), only a few withered flowers – and a banana.

* Nickname for Francesca.

* Our daughters were away in New York, attending a performance of *The Merchant of Venice* at Lincoln Center, with Dustin Hoffman as Shylock, when, in shock, they heard the news of this death.

ACKNOWLEDGEMENTS

I would like to thank, first of all, Erika Tophoven, whose help was invaluable; Alba Branca and Noga Arikha, for their close reading; Ron Costley, Paul Keegan, Frank Pike, and Kate Ward at Faber and Faber for their attention and care; Edward Beckett, John Beckett, Steve Berg of the *American Poetry Review*, Jocelyn Herbert, James Knowlson, Orhan Memed, Emmanuel Moses, and Marcello Simonetta, who were helpful in one way or another; and, most indispensably, for his oft-tried patience and devotion, Avigdor Arikha.